T...

BEATS ‖N RIFT

Natalie
Thks!

BY KER DUKEY

Rifts in Beat
Copyright © 2014 Ker Dukey
Published by Ker Dukey

ISBN-13: 978-1499658576
ISBN-10: 1499658575

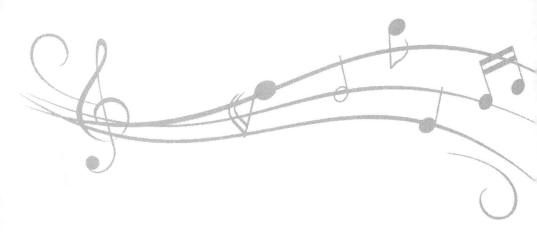

To the lovers who found the lyrics to your song.
Sing, even when the beat gives out.

Torn to follow one soul, when tethered to another, my heart still
beating for its lost lover.
My mind tracing memories so I can breathe, to teach me how to
live when your air can just leave.
Time still moves, the season pass, life flows forward but my heart
remains in the past.
Echoes of our song, the scent on the breeze, everything reminds
me, I'm chasing your shadow as it flees.
Your love devoured me, wrapped me in its soul, than tore itself
from me, left me in despairs dark hold.
A song without lyrics, a beat without sound, a soul with-out its
mate, frayed and dying on the ground.

Thank you to my fans, I write these for you. Strap
on your helmet, I'm taking you on another ride.

Prologue

MEADOW

FRIEND REQUEST FROM JUSTIN JACOBS

ACCEPT   DECLINE

"NO WAY! 'HE is already Facebook requesting? That's surprising."

I look up from the laptop into the bloodshot eyes of my best friend leaning over my shoulder, her minty breath tickling the skin on my cheek.

"So," she continues, "what was he like?"

I slam the laptop closed and stand. "I need to shower." My voice is strained, still suffering from the drinking and singing (moaning) of the night before.

"Oh come on, Meds. I got so drunk I stuck my tongue down that guitarist's throat then threw up on his shoes. I need to live hot, dirty, sex through you."

I turn to my best friend, holding back a laugh at her attire; one sock, her brother's basketball shorts rolled a million times at the waist, and her bra. "He was a deserter like always."

Her brow furrows and she sips from the cup she's holding. "Like always? I don't understand. Didn't you just meet him last night?"

"It's a long, complicated story, Crystal. I'm tired, hung over and I need to ice my knuckles."

She walks towards me, handing me her cup. I sip at the strong coffee, sucking it into my mouth like I'll never be given the chance again.

Her eyes widen at my greed for caffeine. "You want me to start a drip?" she quips with a raised eyebrow.

I squint my eyes and flip her the bird.

"We haven't got to check out until two, Meds. Spill your fuck-ing shit, now."

MEADOW

ELEVEN YEARS EARLIER, AGE 13

"GET YOUR BAG, Meadow. I can't be late again," my Mom calls through the door to my small bedroom in our dingy two-bedroom home.

"I'm ready," I call back, picking up my backpack. I unlock the latch on my door and peek my head out to see my Mom standing by the front door, waiting. She's dressed in her usual work wear; a denim skirt showing way too much leg and a thin black t-shirt with **Drew's Bar** splashed across her large chest, the ink cracking from the strain. Her outfit is finished off with high-heeled pumps that are sure to leave her with blisters by the end of her shift.

I hate the summer vacation. When school let out last year I was left at home while she worked, and her 'then' boyfriend came home early one day, drunk, and decided to knock me around when I refused to make his lunch, leaving me with a broken arm and a headache for Mom when she was questioned by the nurse after she lied and told them I tripped and fell. So this year I've been dragged to work with her so I can't get into "anymore" trouble.

I tiptoe down the narrow hall across the stained, brown carpet. Mom rolls her eyes at me. "He's already left, Med. Stop being dramatic."

Her 'now' boyfriend is just as bad as her last, if not worse. He has roaming eyes and occasionally roaming hands. He's subtle about the way he pats my ass to get me to move out of his way, or when he pulls the neck of my blouse and looks at my chest, telling my Mom I should be wearing a bra by now.

My Mom has always been blind when it comes to men. She changes her boyfriend's often, and sometimes entertains more than one at a time. The girls at school bully me because of it, but she's all I have. I never met my Father; my Mom was only sixteen when she had me. Her parents disowned her so she had it rough, and in turn, so did I. But she got me to thirteen. I'm bright, and apart from the broken arm and the latest pervert, I've escaped any real harm, or at least, that's the way I look at it. She puts a roof over our heads, food in our bellies, and in her own way I think she loves me. That's a lot more than some ever have.

I jump into the car and crank up the stereo, humming along. Mom doesn't make conversation, she just joins me in my humming.

We pull up at the bar Mom works at. The clanking of the engine draws attention from a man wearing an expensive-looking suit, arguing with Mom's boss, Drew. He watches Mom as she opens her door by rolling down her window and pulling the handle from the outside.

Our car is a pile of junk; it has more rust than paint color and the doors creak so loud when you open them they could wake the dead. They often wake the neighbor, who lets us know by shouting, "It's called oil, for fuck's sake. Use some!"

In turn my Mom always hollers back, "I could use the grease from your hair! It's called shampoo! Try using some!"

My Mom always gains male attention; she is beautiful. Slim,

pretty features, dark brown eyes and dark chocolate hair. Her bust is large and men seem to notice that first, just like the guy in the suit right now, drooling on his chin. I have my Mom's skin tone and hair color, although mine has natural honey-colored highlights from the sun, and whereas my hair is wavy, Mom's is poker straight. I have Mom's figure and full lips too, but my eyes are a unique blue, almost violet.

I open my door; it creaks loudly like always. I blush from the sound as I notice two boys standing next to Drew. They look my age and they're identical; dark brown hair, tall. I recognize after a brief moment they're from school. The Jacobs twins; popular, good-looking, and wealthy.

I dip my head as I climb out, hoisting my backpack onto my shoulder.

"Fine, Markus. Leave them here, but if Josie comes here and sees them I'm not covering for you again," Drew tells the man, who nods and gets into his expensive silver car without a backwards glance. Drew's eyes trail to us. "Nice of you to show up."

Mom looks at her watch, pokes her chest out and plasters a smile on her face. "Fifteen minutes late. I'll make it up."

Shaking his head he addresses the two boys. "Take Meadow out back and look after her. Don't get into trouble."

"Why do we have to hang out with the chick?" one of them moans.

Drew blows out a rush of air. "Jared, don't push me today. Just do as you're told."

Mom shoos me in the boys' direction. I walk over to them and nod an acknowledgment.

"Come on then," the other boy commands, taking my backpack from my shoulder.

"What's in the bag?" Jared asks.

I look at him sheepishly. "Just some paper."

He arches an eyebrow. "Why do you have paper?"

"I like to write."

The other boy, the one carrying my bag, keeps staring at me, making me fidget. He brings me to a halt by moving so close into my face I can feel his breath hit and disperse against my skin.

My eyes hold his as they bore into me. "You have purple eyes," I break his gaze. "They're violet, actually."

Jared walks over to me, tilting my head with his finger under my chin, and studies my face.

"Wow, they really are. We aren't the only ones with a unique eye color, brother."

I grip his elbow, mimicking his attention to my eyes. His eyes are an amber color; golden with specks of orange. They remind me of autumn. He smiles at me coyly, making me blush and release my hold on him.

"So what do you like to write about? I'm Justin by the way," the other twin says with a smile. I notice when Justin smiles he doesn't have dimples, unlike Jared.

"Erm, lyrics. I write lyrics." I snap my eyes from Jared's probing gaze.

"No shit!" He chirps, "Well, seems like unique eyes isn't the only thing we have in common. Do you play an instrument?"

I shake my head. "I always wanted to learn guitar but my Mom could never afford to buy me one." I shrug and take a seat under a huge tree situated at the back of the bar in a field of tall grass. When the wind kisses the tips it makes a ripple like a wave in the sea.

Justin drops my backpack next to me, bringing my attention back to him. "So, what school do you go to?"

I flinch as if his words physical struck me with an obscure lash, completely embarrassed that he doesn't even know we go to the same school and share a few classes. Even though I try not to stand out and I sit in the back of my classes, it's still mortifying to be that invisible.

"Our school," Jared answers for me. Justin's eyes widen.

"Really?"

I nod in agreement. "I'm not popular," I mutter. He looks at me, sheepishly.

"Can I read some of your stuff?" Jared asks, breaking the uncomfortable embarrassment.

"Sure." I zip open my backpack and hand some of my papers to him. It's actually nice having someone to show them to. Mom faked interest but that got old when I reached nine and was singing, trying to get her attention, and she called out for me to turn down the radio. I didn't own a radio.

"So, your Mom works for our uncle, huh?" Justin asks.

"If your uncle is Drew, then yes." I smile, and he returns it with a smile of his own. I shift, nervous from his attention. "So, why are you two stuck here on a day like this?"

"You mean hot?" Jared asks. I shrug off my sweater, letting my skin breathe. Both boys have their eyes on me and I feel my skin tinge pink with a blush. I tug the front of my tank top up so it covers the top of my blossoming bust they are both shamelessly checking out.

"Our Mom forces our Dad to take the last two weeks off work every summer to give his undivided attention to us. He lasts two days tops then dumps us here for rest of the time." Jared grins, unfazed by his Father's blow off.

"Don't be an ass. Something just came up. He doesn't like leaving us, but his work is demanding," Justin counters.

"That's why she makes him take the time *OFF WORK*."

It's hard to believe these two are my age, we all seem to of grown up quicker than we should.

Justin rolls his eyes. "It's only one day, he won't do this again, and he has loads planned for these two weeks. Just ignore Jared. He and Dad don't get along."

That statement piques my interest. "But you do?"

He laughs. "We may look alike but we're very different."

Shrugging slightly, I look to Jared who's tapping out a beat on his knee and mumbling lyrics from the pages I gave him. "Well I like you both" I murmur quietly to myself.

OVER THE NEXT two weeks, the three of us bonded. Jared taught me guitar, and when he wasn't teaching me, I played ball with Justin. When the last day rolled around, I was actually sad summer was over and I wouldn't be spending time with them anymore. I'd learned that, outside of the social dynamics of high school, these popular boys were easy to talk to, approachable and fun.

"So, we'll see you at school," Jared tells me, hugging me.

"Sure." I smile weakly, knowing how different our school positions are. Seeing them and actually having them talk to me was unlikely. Passing them in the halls and nodding in acknowledgement was probably how far our friendship would go from here.

MEADOW

FIRST DAY BACK and it already sucked big time. Mom was late getting up; her creepy boyfriend had spent the night. A shiver ghosts through me, remembering having to wear earphones to block out their wails of passion.

I shake my thoughts away and continue yanking at the lock on my locker, sighing in frustration when it won't open. Why do I always end up with the stiff one? I groan as Melissa approaches.

"Nice top, skank," she spits, sniggering. Her friends all mimic her like clones. I close my eyes and count to ten.

I try to stay undetectable as much as possible at school. I hate attention of the boy variety since we turned old enough to notice the opposite sex and Melissa's boyfriend asked me out and sent Melissa into 'Hate Meadow' over-drive. She spread rumours about me and informed everyone about my Mom's promiscuous ways. Since then I cover my entire body in baggy clothes. Thanks to Melissa's hate for me I've been placed at the bottom of the high school food chain.

Boys don't ask me out anymore and I'm happy with that, we were too young for dating anyway in my eyes. My goal is to do well in school and gain a scholarship out of here.

I bang the locker door in defeat.

"At least you can keep some things closed, skank" Melissa grins and I continue my count, way surpassing ten.

"Melissa, not all girls are like you. Leave her alone"

My heart begins to flutter wildly against my chest at the sound of Jared's voice.

"Bite me, Jared,"

"No thanks, I don't snack off my brother's plate."

Her eyes flash with rage. She slams the locker next to me and saunters off with her clan in tow.

"Are you having problems with your locker, Beats?" He had been calling me Beats for the last week, saying I make him need to tap out beats. He plays guitar but his passion is the drums.

"Yeah it's stuck." My eyes meet his and a sigh escapes my lips. I'm grateful he showed up. "You didn't have to say anything to Melissa. I can handle her."

He rattles the lock and slams his palm against it. A clicking resonates in the air and my locker pops open.

"Beats, she was being mean. She's been chasing me and my brother around forever, she shouldn't call people names. Plus, you're my buddy. There's no way I can let her get away with that."

I slip my books into the locker and close it. He stays at my side as I walk to class; a small smile refuses to leave my face at his statement and presence next to me. My smile grows as Justin approaches us. He seems happy to see me, giving me a shoulder squeeze before turning to his brother and punching him in the arm.

"What did you say to Mel? She screeched at me down there, something about you and then stormed off" He looks down the hall in the direction he came from and looks back at us wide eyed shaking his head.

"She was being a bitch to Beats."

Justin looks to me. "You okay?"

I nod and hope the heat crawling up my body isn't visible to them.

"Fair enough. Beats, you want to come over to our place after school?"

I look up and down the hall. Of course, all eyes are on us. My social status climbing the invisible ladder in everyone's minds.

"Okay, sure," I agree, with a little oomph in my voice.

"Good stuff. Meet us in parking lot."

MEADOW

AFTER THAT DAY we became inseparable; the boys took me under their wing. I spent every day with them, and if one was busy the other never was, so I always had one of them to hang with.

They bought me my own guitar for my fourteenth birthday; Jared and I wrote songs together. I called him Rift because he inspired my rifts. When I first told him this he laughed so hard he actually cried. When I asked what was funny he informed me I had mistaken the word, and in fact it is guitar *Riff* but it was too late. Rift stuck and that was what I called him. My nickname, Beats, was used by everyone except for Justin. He would call me either, Beats or Meadow depending on his mood.

The twins were so different in personalities, but so close as brothers. Jared was a musician. He was rougher around the edges, and he was into rock and heavy metal. Justin was a high school dream; he played football, dated the popular girls, and had good grades. The dynamics of their home life reflected this. Their Dad, Markus, was all for Justin. He was into the football dream and pushed Justin hard. Their Mom, Josie, on the other hand, had a soft spot for Jared, and Jared's adoration for her was evident whenever they were in the same space. She also loved having me there but their Dad didn't. He wouldn't speak to me and often I caught him glaring at me. He, like everyone else, assumed there was more to my relationship with his boys than just kids being friends. I heard him talking about the apple not falling far from the whore tree once to Josie, but I ignored it because the truth was, for the first two years of our friendship there really was nothing more to my relationship with them.

I loved them both. They changed my life, made me feel worthy and not trashy the way everyone else had always treated me. But things were about to change.

"HEY, GUYS," BEATS says, walking into the music room where me and my band are practicing a new song. I had asked her to go over the lyrics last night. Her pretty hair sways over her shoulders, and her violet eyes find mine. God, she's cute. Not just in the *I'm a teenage boy and every girl with tits now grabs my attention* cute. She is, without a doubt the prettiest girl in the school and I've crushed on her from the first day she handed me her lyrics. Just looking at her makes me tap out a new beat. She's my muse but she's so scared of being judged by her mother's reputation, she never dates. She hides her figure under baggy clothes; to this day I don't really know what type of figure she has. She won't wear makeup, not that she needs to because her face is perfect. I've admired, loved and protected her, while being what she needs - a friend. Every time I kiss my sort of girlfriend, I see Beats in my mind. I know that's shitty but she doesn't see me or anyone that way, so I have no chance with her. When Jess asked me out in front of all our group of friends, I couldn't really say no. We had been make out partners for a few months, but I'm in love with Beats, so I kill time with Jess. I may be young but I know how I feel, puppy love or not, It was still love.

"Hey, Rift. I rewrote a couple of the lines in the chorus but apart from that it's really good."

She smiles and my heart skips like a pussy-whipped choir boy.

"So, who's the lucky girl, Jess?" she asks about my lyrics.

I grin; her innocence is so adorable. I want to kiss her and snuggle her at the same time. She's had a hard home life and that has made her tough. She learned from me how to handle herself. I taught her self-defence after I went to pick her up from her house one day and her Mom's boyfriend had his son around, and he was pushing Beats around for being frigid. I kicked his ass but wanted her to learn how to do it herself.

She's close to me and my brother, but she's more like me. She shares my personality, we're two sides of the same coin. We love the same music and films, we like to push boundaries and when I manage to get her to open up her inner minx, she follows me into whatever adventure I cook up for the day. One time I convinced her I could drive the digger that was left on a work site at school. I hot-wired the machine and she rode that digger with me even when I admitted I couldn't control it, and we ended up in a ditch and had to run from site security. She's bright and works hard at school. She's relying on getting a scholarship so she's reluctant to let her wild side out too often. I have to coax it out of her most of the time but when I do, she's fantastic.

"What makes you think it's just one?" I smirk, and she slaps my shoulder and rolls her eyes.

"You will leave a wake of broken hearts in this school, Jared Jacobs," she mutters.

I tap out a few beats as she turns on her heels and hurries out the room.

"Beats," I call just before she closes the door. She turns to me. "I'll take your heart with me when I go."

Her laugh rings out into the room. "You better. I can't be left here bleeding in your memory."

Damn, that chick can write lyrics that go straight to my heart.

The door clicks shut behind her retreating form.

"Dude, put your tongue away. Just ask her out already."

My head snaps round to Luke. I had almost forgotten my band members are even here; no one has ever caught on to the fact I have feelings for Meadow. They think I see her as a sister of sorts and even with my subtle hints, like telling her I'll take her heart with me, she just shrugs it off like I don't mean anything real behind it.

"What?" I ask, my voice shaking slightly.

"Drake. He has a thing for Beats. He almost drooled on his guitar."

I snap my eyes to Drake who's flipping the bird. "Eat shit, Luke."

"Man, you've been drooling over her for long enough. Ask her out."

"She doesn't date," I state.

They both look up at me. "She might now. No one's had the balls to ask her out since she told Mason no in front of the whole cafeteria, but that was years ago. Things change. Drake, you should ask her to the dance."

My heart races erratically, even though I'm confident she won't accept his invitation. The small possibility that she might has my head spinning and my body tense. I know Drake likes her, but I never worried about it before now.

"Can we finish up here? I'm starved," I say, trying to change the path of the conversation.

"Yeah, me too. Come on, let's see what lyrics she changed."

Meadow is my co-writer; she always knows how to make the right changes to my lyrics. We're a team and when she's ready to date, it will be me she dates.

"HEY," I CALL as I open the front door to our house.

I love our house, and Mom takes great pride in keeping it immaculate. The plush cream carpets are steam cleaned once a week to keep their color. The white kitchen and bathroom are always spotless and the living space is hardly ever used as there are just too many rooms to use them all, but the rich warm colors on the walls give the vast space a homely feel.

"Hey, baby." Mom smiles.

She hasn't been herself lately. She and Dad have been arguing more often. I found a bruise on her wrist last week. She swore on her life it wasn't from him, but his temper has been flaring more lately, even in front of Justin and me so I know it must be worse when we aren't around to witness it. The way he looks at Mom makes my stomach coil. He has no love in his eyes for her; more like she's dirt from his shoe. Justin doesn't share my concern. In his eyes our Dad is God and can do no wrong. That is what has always separated us.

"Hey, Mom. You look nice."

Her smile widened. "Your Dad's taking me out."

"Really?" The surprise is evident in my tone but she says nothing. She kisses my cheek and then hurries out of the front door.

Justin is at practice, and Beats has to pick her Mom up from the bar so she's coming over later. I kick my shoes off, grab a soda, and go to shower the day off. I stay in there longer than normal, the water scalding my skin. I switch the shower off and wrap a towel around my waist, opening the door that leads to my room.

This is where I find Beats lying on my bed with an arm flung over her face. Her chest is rising and falling in rhythm to her sighing

"Hey."

She lifts her arm, mumbling a weak "Hey."

"What's wrong, Beats?"

"Yo, Jared! You home?" Justin's voice booms.

"Yeah, man. In my room."

His footsteps carry down the hall before he saunters into my room.

"Hey, you want pizza?" he asks, turning to see Beats lying on my bed in a world of her own. He gestures towards her with a head nod. "What's with her?"

I shrug, tapping her leg with my foot. She sighs, sitting up with her dramatic flair. She squirms a little and a blush creeps up her cheeks when she takes in my attire. I almost forgot I'm only wearing a towel. Her eyes scan my body with curiosity. I feel the heat from her eyes burn my skin with every inch of me she absorbs.

"What's up?" Justin asks, breaking her concentration. He sits down next to her, slinging an arm over her shoulder.

"Drake asked me to the dance," she rushes out in almost a whisper.

My stomach knots. Justin smiles up at me nervously. "And?"

"I said yes." She speaks softly, biting her bottom lip as she finishes.

My head spins and the room tilts. She said yes? I want to punch something, preferably Drake's face.

Her eyes shift from me to Justin.

"That's great, babe. About time," He tells her. I debate punching him instead. A whiny noise crawls from the back of her throat as she throws herself back on my bed, gaining a chuckle from Justin.

"So, what's the big deal, Beats? Spill."

"I'm nervous! I've never been out on a date before and I know what you boys are like."

I clear my throat. "You're worried he might want something from you?"

She looks up at me from behind her hand that's now covering her eyes and nods.

"Beats, me and Justin will break his fucking arms off if he tries that shit on you," I tell her, already planning a way to stop this date.

Justin nodded his head in agreement. "Drake's not really like that though."

She groans, sitting back up to look him in the eye.

16

"I like him. I want to kiss him but I'm nervous because I'm not experienced and I know he is."

The bile in the back of my throat burns as it makes its way up. Justin pats her knee, both are seemingly oblivious to my brain exploding inside my head.

"Kissing is easy, just go with the flow," he reassures her.

"My first kiss sucked. The girl was all saliva and teeth," I say.

Her eyes grow wide and I have to dodge the incoming assault from the rolled up pair of socks Justin throws at me.

"Way to make her feel relaxed about it, man." The socks bounce off the wall and land back at his feet.

"Teach me," she murmurs.

I'm sure my eyes are the size of saucers right now. Who is this new girl taken over the body of our timid, never been kissed, never been on a date and was happy about that Beats?

Justin's cough and choking brings my attention to him. "Teach you?"

"Yes, show me how. Let me practice."

"Fine I'll teach you," I quickly reply before Justin can, feeling my body heat with anticipation. Her eyes narrow on me.

"Not you, Rift. You have a girlfriend, that wouldn't be fair to her. I meant Justin." The heat in my body fizzles and is replaced with ice shards. Justin's eyebrows are in his hairline.

"Beats, your first kiss is meant to be special,"

Her laughter startles him. "Well Jared's didn't sound special, and you are special to me, so just teach me. I don't want to suck or crumble into a nervous heap if he tries to kiss me."

She pleads in her cute voice that has gotten her what she wants from us since the day we met her. He looks up at me then back to her.

"Okay, fine. Of course I will."

She beams at him, turning her body towards him.

"Now?" he stutters.

She laughs again, shaking her head in confusion. "Why not?"

17

I clench my fists so hard my knuckles turn white.

Justin shrugs. "Okay, just relax and copy what I do."

He moves towards her, putting his hands on her hips and leaning forward. His lips brush hers, he adds more pressure before pulling back slightly. I can't believe I'm watching myself kiss her, only it's not me. It's my mirror image, my freaking brother kissing the girl I love!

"Open your mouth," he whispers.

Dipping his tongue, hers swipes out to meet his. Her hands press against his shoulders as she turns her head for better access. They look awkward.

"Enough!" I shout, making them both jump apart.

Striding towards her, my hand grasping the nape of her neck, I pull her to her feet. Bringing my other hand to clasp her cheek, I crush my lips down onto her soft, warm mouth. I caress her lips, coaxing them to part with a flick of my tongue. She opens willingly, her tongue meeting my own with hunger. My skin heats as her hands slide up my back, igniting my lust further. When she moans into my mouth I want to write a song about the sound of that moan. Pulling away reluctantly, we're both left panting.

"You don't need to be nervous, Beats. You're an amazing kisser, but these lips are meant for me, not Drake."

Her violet eyes are glazed, her chest still rising and falling with each needy gulp for air. She stares at me for what feels like hours before Justin breaks the spell.

"I guess your plans for the dance have changed." He chuckles.

"What about Jess?" she asks in a whisper.

"She's not you. I've waited long enough for you to be ready to date, there's no way in hell I'm letting it be with someone who isn't me."

"Okay," she murmurs. Just like that!

"I'm going to go order pizza," Justin informs us, leaving us alone. I haven't taken my eyes from hers.

"You okay with this, Beats?"

She bites her lip. Her teeth push down into it making me groan a little; I brush my thumb over the plump red lip, releasing it from her attack.

"Kiss me again," she breathes. So I do, and I don't stop from that day on.

MEADOW

"YOU'RE SIXTEEN NOW so I thought you might like that." I look back down at the present my Mom deemed appropriate for my sixteenth birthday.

She walks into the kitchen, leaving her slimy boyfriend to slide up next to me. His heated morning breath stains my cheek with a hot mist as he whispers into my ear. "You can model them for me any time."

Swallowing the vomit trying to force its way up from his disgusting suggestion, I shift in my seat to move away from him. I'm surprised he's here. When I woke up last night he wasn't the one occupying my Mom's bed. I'd needed the bathroom, and tip toeing quietly across the landing I'd knocked straight into the hard chest of Jared and Justin's Dad. Air left my lungs as shock settled in my stomach. Why would he be here with my Mom? He hated me because to him, I was lower class, my Mom was someone he spoke about in harsh whispers, yet he was in her room with her doing God knows what. Before I could speak he'd pinned me against the wall. "If you tell my boys I was here, I will force them to never see you again. Do you hear me?" he had snarled with hatred, his spit spraying my face, his hands so tight on my arms I was sure I would be left with bruises.

I hate the way their Dad treats me. On the rare times he

acknowledges me, it's with pure revulsion in his eyes, even though his eyes have begun to roam my body now I'm getting older. I'm positive the more he looks at me, the more he hates me for his own perverseness.

Mom saunters back into the room, dragging me from my thoughts.

"God, Meds. You could be grateful instead of being such a prude. I'm not stupid, you know? I've seen how you and Jared are together. I'm not naïve enough to think you two don't sleep together."

Her boyfriend's eyes were glued on me. I shudder as his mind unclothes me. "Actually, Mom, we don't. I'm too young for that."

Her boyfriend's groan has Mom's eyes darting to him. "Don't let her fool you, Brian. She's been messing with those boys since she was thirteen."

I get up, desperate to escape. "Thanks for this, Mom."

I scurry down the hall and into my room, holding up the thread of lace she called underwear. I stuff it into the back of my closet. She's wrong about me and Jared. We are all over each other because we love each other with a passion I've never known or seen before. His love was like oxygen to me and I was always gasping for breath, I live and breathe him. He's the last thought in my mind at night, and my first thought when I wake up. We write songs together, play together, study together, laugh together. We're inseparable, just like we always have been, except now we kiss and touch. We were waiting before we took our relationship further. Waiting for my sixteenth birthday. Waiting for today.

Dressing quickly, I hurry out of the house.

WHEN I GET to school, Jared and Justin are waiting for me, their grins infectious. Jared and I had added violet streaks to our hair at the weekend, and he looks so rock God today, sporting low rise jeans, boots, a long sleeve black t-shirt and a chain hanging from a loop of his jeans. Rushing towards me, he picks me up into an embrace, swinging me around.

"Happy birthday, beautiful." His lips crush against mine, my legs wrapping around his waist, my arms around his neck.

"Put her down, Jared. PDA much?" Justin gags.

We giggle into each other's mouths. Jared slides me down his body until my feet touch the floor. I'm grabbed by my arm and spun to face Justin. Picking me up, he squeezes me tight. Returning his embrace, I struggle for breath. "Happy birthday, Beats."

"Thank you."

He releases me with a grin. Jared's hand slips into mine. "So, this is from both me and Justin." He places a long black velvet box in my palm. My eyes flash to him then Justin, gaining a chuckle from them.

"Open it."

Snapping the box open, my vision is filled with a beautiful necklace lying against black velvet. I gulp past the lump forming in my throat. Jared takes the box, pulling the chain free.

"The charms speak for themselves,"

The rope chain has three charms dangling from the centre. "The guitar is you."

He kisses me as he lifts the chain over my head and around my neck. Justin points to the football. "Obviously that's me." He grins.

I move the charms through my fingers. "The drum is you," I whisper, throwing myself into Jared's chest, climbing his body to wrap myself around him. He sighs into my neck, his arms securing me to him.

"Our Dad's going away on business for the night, so Mom said we can have a few people over. I was hoping you would crash at our place."

A smile lifts my lips, and I nod. Justin walks away swearing under his breath as Jared's lips attack mine.

THE DAY PASSES in a blur of classes, well wishes, and daydreams of what the night will mean for us. I can't wait to give myself completely to Jared. He owns me already, and this will cement that. The anticipation leaves me lightheaded.

After school we hit the supermarket for snacks and drinks. Justin left to go to football practice; he has an important game approaching so the coach is riding him hard, making the team do extra practice.

As Jared drives me home to get an overnight bag, his eyes keep gliding over to me, a coy smile gracing his full, suckable lips, making me squirm in my seat.

Pulling up outside my house my stomach twists, and not in a good way.

"What the fuck?"

"Oh, God. Rift, let's just go to your house," I whisper.

His head turns to me. "Beats, that's my Dad's car." He points, confusion evident in his tone.

"Yeah, I know. If he sees you driving he will get mad at you, so let's go."

He shakes his head. "He's meant to be out of town. If he's come over here he must be looking for me or he would be at Justin's practice. Shit! Maybe it's Mom, she's been acting so weird lately."

I'm mute, anxiety making me shake.

He pops the door open, jumping out. Adrenaline flushes through my veins. Opening my door I rush from his truck, grabbing his arm, trying to stop him racing up the path to my house.

"Rift, please." My voice is barely a whisper. He looks down at me then to my firm hand on his arm. He senses it, right in this moment. His eyes flutter as the pain of betrayal in my face registers to him. I feel it in the air around me as his expression changes from concerned, to suspicious, to angry.

"What the fuck is going on, Beats?"

He doesn't let me answer, pulling free from my grasp and opening my front door with ease. She was never one for safety or privacy, my mother. He rushes down the dingy, badly lit hallway. I follow, tears already flowing down my cheeks. The chorus of loud sex; my Mom moaning and his Dad grunting fills the silence between us. The house is small and the walls are thin. I'm used to hearing my Mom, she isn't shy. But watching the color drain from Jared's face leaves me ashamed of who I am, of whose I am.

"You fucking knew. How could you look me in the face every day?"

My stomach jolts. "I… I'm so...rry, Rift."

His eyes are cold, pure ice replacing the heat I usually find there. Pushing past me with force, he leaves me staring after him.

"Wait! Please don't leave me!" A choked sob escapes me.

He doesn't even turn around when he mutters, "We're done."

Collapsing to the ground from the weakness in my knees, I gasp for air. Mom's door opens, and Mr Jacobs looks out and sees Jared's back as he slams the door closed.

He rushes me, gripping me around the throat and dragging me up from the floor then slamming me hard against the wall. My head collides with the cheap plaster, denting it. I struggle for breath, his image blurring from the build-up of tears. The smell from his sweaty naked form seeps into my nose making me want to gag but I can't do anything his squeezing my throat tighter. He can kill me, it doesn't matter. I can't go back to being the girl before Jared and Justin. I can't survive without them in my life, not after knowing what it's like to have them. My love for Jared is what powers my body. How can I function without his love in return?

"You fucking bitch. I told you what would happen if you told my boys."

I try shaking my head but it's no good. The walls close in around me, fog clouding my mind, and then darkness steals me.

Justin

WORKOUT WITH COACH was killer. Every muscle aches but it will be worth it. Dad has already been talking with scouts and colleges that are interested in me. He keeps me focused with his belief I'm going all the way.

I make it home around nine, expecting people to already be here, or at least be arriving. I notice the drive has only Mom's truck on the forecourt. I'm surprised but relieved I can shower and change before people get here.

Opening the front door, I almost knock straight into Jared, our faces an inch apart. He's pale and his eyes are downcast. The hairs on my neck rise. "What's wrong with you?"

"We're leaving." He speaks with authority, like it isn't a choice, it's happening. I follow him as he anxiously gathers suitcases and piles them at the front door. My whole body goes rigid.

"What's going on, Jared? Where's Beats?"

"Fuck Beats."

I actually flinch and stumble backwards with the venom in his voice. "What did you say?"

Stopping in front of me, his face contorts in disgust. "Dad's been fucking her Mom and Beats knew. He's also been knocking Mom about and threatened her life. I'm taking her out of here. I never should have let it get this far. I knew she wasn't right."

Shock settles in at what he's saying; the room spins. When I finally refocus I reach out for him, stopping him from getting more stuff.

"Jared, seriously. What the hell? Dad would never hurt Mom. She's been depressed, she doesn't realize what she's saying."

Shoving me backwards with a snarl he carries on moving things. "I knew you would stick up for him. I just caught him in the act, Justin."

I shake my head. "Caught him doing what exactly?"

Jared's temper is like a fire cracker and I can see it blowing. "I caught him fucking Beats' whore of a mother."

I mind can't keep up, my Dad wouldn't do that and Jared worships Beats and has never, ever put down her mother or her. Nothing was making sense. Our Dad couldn't stand Meadows Mom. "Where is Beats?"

His glare penetrates me, pinning me to the spot. "Are you listening to me? Dad's fucking her Mom and hitting ours. I left Beats where she belongs, with her mother. I'm taking Mom away from here, Justin. You coming or not?"

"Don't be stupid. Where are you going to go?"

"I don't care but I'm leaving now. I'm not sitting around here waiting for him to beat the shit out of her."

He brushes past me and out the front door, loading Mom's truck. Headlights beam up the drive, highlighting us in a glow.

Dad leaps from his car. "What are you doing?" he bellows at me. I shrug my shoulders and hold my hands up.

"Jared's packing up and leaving with Mom." I almost want to laugh at the absurdity, this couldn't be happening. Disbelief settles itself in my bones unmoving, letting me watch everything play out as if it wasn't happening to us.

Jared throws another suitcase into the truck then turns to me.

"You're not coming?" His voice is strained. He's serious, he's really going to leave.

"No, he's not and you're not leaving either. You have the wrong idea. I was only at Meadow's house to speak to her Mom."

Jared's laugh is ice cold. "Yeah, sounded like talking. What about Mom?" He squares up to Dad, flexing his neck, his hands balling into fists. "The bruises? Dad?"

"Your Mom's depressed. She's been brainwashing you."

Shaking his head and walking back into the house. He appears a minute later with Mom, helping her into the truck and shutting her door. "Justin, get in the truck," he commands.

"No way is he leaving, Jared. He has a game on Friday. You're being ridiculous, and you're really pushing my patience."

He ignores Dad and looks at me. "I'm not coming back, Justin. Come with us, please."

I shake my head. Where will he go? He isn't old enough to just take off. He'll be back when he cools off. He'll never leave Beats or me.

"I can't. I have a game."

"Fuck the game. Get in the truck."

I step back and Dad's hand lands on my shoulder. "My life's the game, Jared," I tell him, hoping he will understand. I can't risk missing the game for his tantrum.

Pain washes into his eyes, distorting the color, but it's fleeting. Anger replaces it as he gets in the truck and leaves.

It isn't just a tantrum.

Justin

"MY DAD'S NOT going to be there, Meadow. And even if he was, he's been better with you lately. Come on! I can't have a party without you there."

It's been nearly two years since Jared left with my Mom. There has been no letters and no phone calls. Nothing.

When Meadow turned up late that night and I had to tell her Jared took off, she broke. I had to hold her while she sobbed. She was inconsolable. It was so hard on her; she lost weight, stopped playing her guitar, stopped writing.

After the first three months, when it became apparent to both of us he wasn't coming back, we bonded even tighter. She wouldn't leave my side. I knew being near me made her feel closer to Jared. In a way, being close to her made me feel closer to him too.

She became more involved in school, came to my every game and practice. She stopped dying colors into her hair. Her style changed; she dressed more like the popular girls. She studied extra hard and went back to not dating. Not that guys didn't ask her out, they did. She had blossomed even more in the last two years. Now she wears more fitted clothes showing off her figure; full bust, trim waist, shapely hips and toned long legs. She's perfect and I'm still completely in love with her. I've been in love with her since the day I looked into her unique eyes when she was thirteen years old. But she was off limits then. She didn't date, and when she decided to date, my brother snapped her up. He never knew how much I loved her but I could feel his love radiating from him since the day we met her, so I always knew I wouldn't pursue her and she would be with him. I smiled and supported them when they became an item. But he's gone and the need for her has gotten stronger than ever.

"Okay, fine. I'll come but you have to promise to not disappear with Melissa."

I look over at her, surprised. Melissa is my hook-up buddy. She has been since forever. She's easy and she worships me. Sometimes I need to feel needed in that way.

"Are you jealous, Meadow?" I grin at her arched brow before she retorts.

"No, it's just annoying being forced to parties then being left by ten o' clock so you can go get some with the school 'ho."

I laugh loud at her little outburst. "That happened once, Meds, and you were fine being swamped with admirers fighting for your attention." I arch my own brow at her.

"Hardly, anyway I'm not interested in them."

Her voice is small. I put my hand on her knee, sneaking looks at her while trying to concentrate on the drive to her house.

"Meadow," I breathe. She turns her head to look out the window. She sends me mixed signals all the time. Sometimes she sounds like she's jealous, but she never takes things further. I'm terrified if I do try to take things from more than friends, she will shut me down and I'll lose her altogether. I couldn't cope if I lost her.

When Jared left and didn't come back, I felt like half the guy I used to be. He's my brother, my best friend. I still struggle with the fact he never came back. Just looking in the mirror is painful.

I pull up and she jumps out; the tension in the car is at an all-time high. She's in and out in minutes, her overnight bag on her shoulder. Pulling open the door she throws it in the back seat. She grins. "Let's go, birthday boy."

And just like that the tension evaporates.

29

MEADOW

"SO, DO YOU call him Jared when you're making out?"

I'm ready to punch this girl in the face and I'm not one for violence. He has been gone two years and stupid drunk dumbasses still bring him up like he's still here. Nobody else saw the Jacobs twins as individuals, even after Jared upped and left. The pain still surfaces when people talk about him, even after all this time. What people don't realize is that to me, Justin is nothing like Jared. They're completely different. I don't see Jared when I look at Justin, which is crazy because they share a face, but I know both of the boys better than anyone so I've always seen them as the amazing individuals they are… were.

I clutch at the hum beginning in my chest; the sorrow that lives there is a constant ache, a soul crying out for its lost mate.

"I don't call him anything because we don't make out." I roll my eyes as hers bulge.

"Oh, God! Is that why he cheats on you all the time?"

I really want to kill Justin for leaving me after he promised he wouldn't.

I look around the swarms of sweaty classmates and spot him pinned up against a wall, Melissa's tongue down his throat. My stomach turns over. I hate that he lets that trollop touch him. I know he has feelings for me, I can see it when he looks at me, and I do for him too but I'm so scared to open my heart again. Especially to Jared's brother. How low would that make me? I know he must feel the same because he's never tried to make a move either.

My eyes lock with his as Melissa lets him up for air. He holds my gaze for what feels like forever, then pushes Melissa aside as she tries leaning back in to him.

"Justin, where are you going?" She whines loud enough to carry over the music as he leaves her. He mounts the stairs, ignoring people as they try to talk to him.

"You a Jesus type?" the idiot standing next to me asks. "I don't think even for God I would be able to keep my hands off him. He's so yummy."

I sigh, closing my eyes to let out an exasperated breath. She's not wrong. Justin is gorgeous. He's filled out into a six foot three, ripped, athletic God. His brown hair neatly styles over his perfect face. He has a strong jawline, full lips, a neat nose and those amazing amber eyes surrounded by thick lashes.

"Excuse me," I tell the drunken girl, moving her to the side and brushing past the sweaty bodies dancing in front of me. I make my way to the stairs and go to Justin's room. I try the door but it's locked so I rap my knuckles against it.

"This room is off limits!"

"It's me. Open the door."

"Meadow, I'm busy getting laid. Go to the spare room to crash."

My stomach turns over. He doesn't ever talk to me like that and I know he wouldn't in front of someone else so he's more than likely not with anyone. But the thought of him in there getting laid leaves an unsettled feeling in my stomach.

"Okay," I call to him. "I was just checking if it's okay if I take someone in there with me?" I bait him, playing him at his own game.

"What?" comes his confused voice, a notch higher than before.

"I thought I'd get laid too, so I just wanted to make sure it was okay to take my guy in there. So... okay, thanks."

I fold my arms over my chest and wait the two seconds it takes for him to yank the door open. His face is pure rage. He looks past me and down the hall.

"WHO?" he bellows. I shake my head and push past him into his room. He keeps looking into the hall.

"I was lying, Justin. You know me better than that."

His head falls forward and his shoulders slump. He slams the door and turns to me. "You shouldn't lie to me, Meadow."

I open my arms to gesture around his room. "Really? But you can lie to me? Who you in here getting laid by?"

He grimaces. "Fine. What do you want?"

"Why are you mad?" I ask, walking over to him. He sighs and brings his hand down over his face then up and through his hair.

"I'm mad that I let Melissa kiss me. I try to lose myself in her."

I reach for his hand, grateful for him opening up. "Why do it then? I hate her, Justin. She's not worthy of you." His eyes trace up from our hands and lock onto mine.

"Because I can't have who I really want," he whispers, furrowing his brow.

"Why can't you?"

He gazes at me in silence for an eternity then closes the distance between our bodies.

His eyes travelling from my own to my mouth; he's asking permission, waiting for me to say okay, so I bring my lips to brush against his. He smells of toothpaste. He must have just brushed.

"Meadow," he whispers. His breath heats my lips, hands grip my hips in a resilient hold. Closing his eyes he murmurs my name again.

"Meadow… don't play with me."

I feel the strain in his hold. I deepen my lips to his, his moan encouraging me. His hands loosen their grip and slide up my back into my hair. Holding me to him, his tongue invading my mouth. I return his kiss with the same intensity he is showing me. Lowering his hands to the hem of my top, he lifts it over my head, breaking the kiss for a second before dropping it to the floor and resuming his touch. Gasping for air, he breaks our kiss again to look down at the flesh he has revealed. My lace bra shows my pert nipples, my breath lifting them with each pant.

"God, Meadow." He cups my face with one hand. "Turn around."

I do as I'm told, turning my back to him. He gathers my hair and lays it over my shoulder while his lips caress the other side, his warm lips tickling the flesh.

He unclasps my bra and slides it down my arms, and I tremble with nerves and anticipation. His breathing hitches when my bra falls, exposing my breasts.

His mouth closes over my pulse beating rapidly against my neck, tongue flicking, caressing, tracing kisses down over my shoulder, continuing to my back and down my spine.

When he reaches the base of my back, he grips my hips and turns me. He's on his knees looking up at me in wonder.

I run my hands through his mussed hair as his lips continue their journey back up my body, travelling up my navel. He dips his tongue into my belly button, eliciting a soft moan.

Getting to his feet, closing a hand over one breast, his thumb brushing over my nipple while bringing his mouth to the other. My breathing accelerates with each flick of his tongue over the tight bud, a stir in my lower stomach telling me I need more. I reach for him, pulling his head up to press my mouth to his; I nip his bottom lip and he jolts away.

"Fuck. You bit me, Med."

I flush with embarrassment. "I'm sorry."

Jared and I had raw passion for each other, an animalistic craving. Biting was something that happened a lot when we made out, but clearly that was just us, and not something that's done when making out. My stomach drops there's a buzzing in my ears as the flames from my embarrassment burns fiercely up my neck Feeling completely mortified I advert my eyes from his.

"It's okay, it just shocked me for a second," he reassures me, bringing his lips back to mine. He slides the top button on my hipster jeans open, lowering the zipper. I gasp as he slides his hand into my panties. Feeling his palm against my bare sex has the wings from the butterflies in my belly fluttering enthusiastically.

"You feel so hot down there, Med." He whispers in awe.

He guides me over to his bed and holds me as he lays me down, covering my body with his own. His lips find my skin again, raining kisses over me, starting at my lips, down my neck, chest, over both breasts and down to my stomach.

He coaxes me to part my legs so he can kneel between them. Gripping the waistband of my jeans he slides them down my hips; I lift so he can move them under my ass. He moans when he exposes my lace panties, his gaze roaming my full body.

"You are unbelievably beautiful, Meadow. I can't believe you hid this perfection for so long."

I reach up for his belt buckle but flinch when the bedroom door flies open.

"Shit!" Justin shouts and lies over my body to cover me, fumbling around to pull the covers from underneath us.

"You fucking asshole. I knew you we're screwing that tramp all this time," Melissa screeches, gathering an audience behind her.

"Get the fuck out, Melissa! Now!" Justin roars at her.

She huffs, storming off and leaving the door open. A couple of Justin's football buddies take up the space in the doorway with shit-eating grins on their faces. I try to cover myself the best I can but I'm pretty exposed.

"Fucking hell, Jacobs. No wonder you didn't want us hitting on her. Wow…weeee!" One whistles making the heat in my cheeks burn brighter.

"You lied, man. You said she didn't put out," the other jock moans, like a child being told he can't have ice cream.

My heart pounds in my chest so loud my jaw tense trying to prevent myself from screaming at them or of breaking down and crying, making the scene even more mortifying. I had completely let myself get caught up in Justin and moving on. Letting myself feel and experience things for the first time since Jared ripped my heart out. I kept telling myself this was a dream, there wasn't half our school about to start gossiping about catching me naked with Justin. The cool air making Goosebumps scatter across my exposed skin and the fact the door was still open, brought the humiliation to form tears. This wasn't a dream no matter how hard I willed it to be.

"Shut my fucking door before I kill you both," Justin commands. They chuckle but comply.

He sighs heavily. "That's not as bad as they made it sound, Meadow. You know I would never talk about you like that."

I smile and gently push him off me swiping the tears before they could fall. I shimmy my jeans up and fasten them, and slip off the bed to locate my discarded clothes, putting them back on.

"Meadow, I just told them we weren't an item when they kept asking. I didn't say anything about you putting out."

"I know. Its fine, Justin."

He jumps up from the bed and grabs my arms. "It's clearly not. Why are you getting dressed?"

I break free from his grasp. "Because the door's not locked and half the party just saw me naked. You might not care but I do."

Sighing and reaffirming his hold on my arms. He hushes out "Of course I care. I don't want anyone seeing you like that. I'm pissed at myself for doing this with you here, with people everywhere."

He tips my chin up so he can look into my eyes. "I've been in love with you since forever and I want us to be together. This should have been special."

My heart thunders rapidly against my chest at his words before I can digest them or reply a commotion and then a hammering on the door steals are attention. Justin's Dad's voice booms through the wood. "I want everyone out and you down stairs in ten minutes."

I'm paralyzed, his Dad's voice pulling the demon from my nightmare into my reality just on the other side of the door.

Justin refocuses on me. "Shit, Meadow. You're shaking, you look sick."

"You said your Dad wasn't coming home tonight."

He releases my arms and begins to fix his belt buckle. "Yeah I didn't think he was."

"I need to leave,"

He looks down at me. "Is this because I said I love you, Meds? Are you running from me?" His tortured look swallows his beautiful features. He has always feared me leaving. I had to work extra hard to make sure my grades were good enough to follow him to his choice of college.

I reach for him, bringing his body against mine. "No, never. Don't think like that." I pull back, looking up into his eyes. "I love you too, I just don't want to be here when your Dad is."

He exhales, releasing the breath he was holding. "Med, you can't blame him forever. Jared left him too, you know? And that shit with my Mom was lies. He would never hit her; he's not a violent man."

After all this time Justin still believes his Dad is a saint. I never told him that he held me up by my throat, leaving dark purple bruises for weeks. I had to wear turtle neck sweaters to hide them.

"Wait" He shakes his head "you said you love me too?"

"I just think we got a little carried away tonight. Maybe we shouldn't rush things. I think I shouldn't stay,"

His eyes darken the tick in his jaw begins to flicker all the signs his agitated. "But you love me too, right, Meds?"

"Yes, I do, and tomorrow we can spend time together and talk more about us okay?"

"Okay."

MEADOW

"IT'S BEEN THREE months since me and Justin became an item and it's a special night. It's his last game of the season. We're skipping prom. I'm going to surprise him," I tell Maria, my closest girlfriend. We're not best friends but we both have boyfriends on the football team so we bonded a little.

"I love it. So, you're not going to the game?" She's doodling her name on her text book, ignoring the written work we're supposed to be doing. As it's the last day of school, no one is doing their work.

"No, it's an away game and I have to help Mom move our shit out before the landlord locks the house up with our stuff inside."

"Where is she moving to?"

I groan, hating to talk about my Mom. "Her boss, Drew, is putting her up for a while."

Maria just nods her head. Everyone knows what my Mom's like and I can't wait to be away from her. This will be my last deed for her and then I'll be gone with Justin to Florida State, hopefully never to return. She had become better over the last year, she wasn't seeing anyone and was making more effort at work but she still didn't really act like a parent. She had never been a loving mother and I only knew the difference of what a mother should be like towards her kids from when Josie was around. But even she left one of her sons.

How can we be so easily discarded, not wanted, a hindrance to the people who made us, carried us in their bodies. Weren't Moms automatically programed to love their kids? I blamed it on the fact she was practically a kid herself when she had me and her maturity seemed to stay at sixteen. I didn't give Josie an excuse because I didn't know what she went through behind closed doors with that horrible man she called a husband. Her leaving weighed heavy on Justin's self-esteem though. They weren't really close but she was still his mother. She and Jared leaving with no contact left its scars.

After sending Justin a text to tell him I'll see him later tonight, I go home to help get Mom moved out. Luckily, Drew is helpful and we have her packed up and moved within three hours. I'm glad I took Maria up on skipping the rest of school after lunch and going for a spa treatment, consisting of a full body wax, including a painful bikini wax. We have a mani/pedi, and our hair washed and styled. My plan is to shower at Justin's then wait naked in his bed for him as his Dad is out of town.

When I arrive, I jolt to a stop, shocked to walk in the front door and straight into a wall of Mr Jacobs.

Stumbling back I mutter an apology. I try side stepping him, but he blocks my path and my heart rate doubles. The echo of his hands on my throat still effecting me after all this time. The choking representing more than just his violence, it was the day part of me died inside.

"You have a key now?" he asks, pinning me with an intolerable glare.

"Justin gave it to me. I'm supposed to meet him here," I croak, and hate myself for sounding weak.

"You're just like your whore of a mother. You thought you'd encourage Jared with the music crap, telling him he could make it big just so you could ride the success train, then when he dumped your ass, you moved on to better things with my Justin. Who did your Mom have to fuck to get you in to Florida State?"

I try to swallow but my mouth has completely dried of all saliva. "I worked hard to get a scholarship." I croak, he's so bitter and calls my Mom whore yet he was sleeping with her. I want to scream at him for being a hypocrite and an asshole, but my fear prevents me from being able to.

"Worked hard? On your back, or was it on your knees? Damn, you must be a good lay to keep my boy interested. He doesn't even look at those other tramps who throw themselves at him."

I hate what he's saying but I'm pleased to hear Justin only has eyes for me; a twisted girl's need to feel special against the hurtful words he's using to describe me.

"You'll ruin his reputation when he goes pro." He looks me up and down and licks his lips, making me quiver with disgust and fear. It's crazy how your body betrays you and turns you back into a defenceless child when the person who plagues your nightmares is standing in front of you. He studies me for what feels like hours before his features smooth out and he nods his head towards the stairs.

"He had a tough day, we got back early. He's in the shower. Tell him I'll be out for most the night." And with that he leaves. My tense muscles relax. His change in mood adding another layer of confusion to the whole situation.

Sucking in much needed oxygen, I ascend the stairs. The shower Is running. I'll have to change my plans around the fact he's home early. I slowly creep into his room, shutting the door and dropping my overnight bag by his bed. There's only a soft glow from his bedside light dancing shadows across the walls, setting a romantic mood. Stripping myself bare, pulling my hair loose and running my hands through it. I gulp down the nerves and walk towards the bathroom door, I stop as it opens. *Crap, there goes joining him in the shower!*

"Fuck," Justin groans as he takes in my naked form. He looks delicious, water dripping down his perfect abs into the towel that's covering his obvious erection. My nipples pebble and I become wet between my thighs.

"We have waited way too long for this. Just take me. I need you to take me," I beg.

Three months of teasing, touching, kissing but not going further has been difficult for both of us and I'm done waiting.

"Don't you want to talk first?" He seems completely thrown by me being here naked. I love him more in this moment. He's always been worried after nearly taking my virginity at a party full of people. He wants to make it special, savor me, but I'm different to him. He's gentle, romantic. I like spontaneous, lustful, and rough around the edges. He also knows Jared left the night I was supposed to give this gift to him, so it's a raw subject and I just want it over with now. Not really a way to think about losing your virginity but that's just how I feel.

"I don't want to talk. I've waited long enough. I need you now. I didn't expect you to be back so I didn't have time to shower. Maybe we should go in there?"

I smile, biting my lip. Lust fills his eyes, and he charges at me, lifting me up and ramming me against the wall, not hard enough to hurt me but with more force than I'm used to from him. His lips ravish mine, taking his kisses down my neck, sucking and biting. I cry out with pleasure from the new, aggressive side to him.

I love that seeing me naked and willing to finally take this step makes him just as lust-crazy as me. He knows I like a firmer touch and he is giving me what I need.

My nipple tingles as he takes it into his mouth and sucks hard.

"Oh God," I cry out, writhing shamelessly against the bulge pressing into me. "I need more."

His finger grazes over my opening. "Shit, you're so wet."

Whipping the towel away and without warning, he plunges straight into me. A gasp escapes me from the pain and abrupt intrusion. Tears overflow my eyes, and I try to cover the whimper leaving me. Stilling his movement, I'm completely filled with him. I feel his balls against the bottom of my ass, he's so deep.

"You're so tight and so perfect," he groans into my neck, oblivious to the cascade of tears I can't hold from falling as he begins to move his hips, thrusting hard, punishingly. The burn retreats from his rude entry and soon pleasure overrules it. I swipe away the tears before he can notice them, the pain subsiding more and more with every tilt of his hips.

He pulls out almost completely before filling me again, almost painfully every time but so good I don't care about the sting. I relish the pleasure/pain he gives me as he continues to move against my body, our sweat-soaked skin caressing against each other's, my hard nipples aching for his mouth. He reads my body perfectly, sucking and lapping at them, grazing his teeth over the tight buds.

My moans are loud, shattering the thick yearning-filled air. My nails rake at his back and shoulders, making him pump his hips into me faster. I'm burning inside and out. My head tilts back and his face burrows into the crook of my neck, our pants and moans in unison.

I push down on him as he thrusts forward, up and down. He feels incredible inside me. My body begins to tense, shocks of pleasure building, racing through my veins. My inner muscles squeeze his length, my blood vibrating in my skin as pleasure stirs deep within my core, spiralling throughout my body.

"Oh, God!"

He follows me, calling out too. His hot come erupts from him inside me.

I cling to him, waiting for my breathing to stabilize. After a few minutes I can finally breathe without shaking. He lowers me to the floor, kissing my forehead.

"I'm sorry I couldn't hold back for longer. I just didn't expect this and got a little carried away. Go shower, then we can talk," he tells me, his breathing still labored. Reaching for his towel to cover himself, he taps my ass and ushers me towards the bathroom.

I walk in slow motion, trying to stay upright on my shaky legs. Closing the door and leaning against it, the smile on my face leaves my jaw aching. Although I'm surprised by the way Justin has just taken me, I'm also happy we finally took that step and he matched my hunger in that department.

I turn the shower on, tying my hair up so it doesn't get wet, and make quick work of cleansing my body. I feel tender in the best possible way. After, I slip into my jeans and a camisole top. The bedroom is empty when I come out of the bathroom. I grab the glasses and champagne from my overnight bag. I brought them to celebrate Justin's last game, but now we have more to celebrate.

I open the bedroom door and hear Justin shouting. My insides curdle at the thought of his Father coming back early and hearing our love making. I rush down the stairs into the kitchen and came to an abrupt stop. A cracking sound rings out into the room as the glasses and champagne slide from my hands and smash onto the floor. I don't hear Justin talking at me. I see his mouth moving but all I hear is my own heartbeat roaring in my ears.

My body moves as Justin shakes me, and slowly his voice penetrates my ears.

"Med, are you okay? Did you cut your feet?"

I shake my head without even knowing the answer. Justin's face is pale, and worry masks his features.

"Why are you wearing that?" I ask, pulling on his dirty jersey. He looks down, confused.

"Because I just came from my game, baby."

"Baby! Seriously?" Jared asks from the other side of the kitchen. He's wearing only jeans, no shirt, and his hair is wet like he's just come out the shower. *Oh, God.*

"Fuck off, Jared. A lot has changed since you bailed on us." Justin sneers.

"Clearly."

Shock. That's what this is. That's why I feel like someone has poured cement into my body, keeping me frozen to the spot. My eyes take Jared in. Oh, God. His hair is longer than Justin's, even slicked back from the shower. After all these years of saying how different they are, I mixed them up! And what a mix up. I want to cry but I don't know what the tears would represent.

"I don't understand." My voice comes out hoarse.

"Well, I'm guessing by the way you're now freaking out, my brother didn't tell you I was coming back."

My gasp is audible. I look to Justin who still looks worried, and now angry.

"I was going to tell you tonight, I only found out yesterday but he beat me here. I thought he was coming tomorrow. My Dad went to get him. After he called us and told me something that should have come from him in person, when it happened not a week later"

"Wait… your Dad knew he was here?"

"Yeah."

That asshole. He set me up to find Jared in the shower thinking he was Justin. I fight back the tears.

"Well, it was a hell of a welcome home." Jared grins.

"Listen, baby, I know this is a shock."

I shake my head. "I can't do this," I mutter, stepping back and running up the stairs to get my shoes and bag.

I hear the footfalls of both of them following me. I rush into Justin's room and gather my things. Justin enters behind me, gripping my arm.

"Where are you going? You're meant to spend the week here before we leave for Florida. And I need you right now Med something happened"

My eyes drift to Jared who leans over Justin's shoulder. "Beats, it's okay. I'm not staying past tomorrow. You can forget you saw me and carry on as normal."

I know he's telling me in a hidden message that we can forget he just fucked my brains out against Justin's bedroom wall.

"Why is there steam in here? Did you use my shower?" Justin turns to Jared.

"Yeah, Dad said mine is broken and that my room is now a

weights room." I hear the bitter undertone in his voice.

"Why did you come back?" I ask.

I feel destroyed all over again just seeing him. Knowing what we just shared is crippling me and the guilt has its own kind of torture. A glass sheen fills his eyes

"Our Mom died. I came to arrange her funeral with Justin," he struggle to say. The grief almost suffocating his words.

"Oh my God, that's awful. What happened?" I cry out. Pain flashes across his eyes.

"She got sick. I thought she had more time. She didn't." His battling with himself to stay strong, to put on this front that he's ok. He would be crushed inside and just like I always have, I could read it in his eyes.

I want to hold them both, grieve with them but I feel torn and confused and angry as hell at Jared and also Justin for keeping this stuff to himself.

"So, how long did you wait before jumping into my brother's bed?" he asks, changing the subject so he doesn't show us weakness. My mouth gapes. Justin turns so fast that by the time I realize what's happening, fists are flying and Justin is straddling Jared's waist, crashing blow after blow into him. My screams fill the air as I try to drag him off but I stand no chance of moving him.

Jared lets Justin hit him; he isn't even trying to block him. "Stop it, STOP IT!" I scream.

"My turn," Jared growls, rolling, forcing Justin down. Jared's fists connect so hard, the cracking sound makes me empty my stomach onto the plush carpet.

"Oh, GOD, PLEASE," I beg. Jared's eyes lock onto me and he jumps from Justin's limp body and rushes to me. I try pushing him away but I'm too weak; his strength easily overpowers me.

He scoops me up like a bride and carries me into the bathroom, resting me down on the counter next to the sink. Turning on the cold tap and wetting a flannel, he dabs at my face as I sit, shaking.

"Get your fucking hands away from her." My eyes find Justin's;

he's standing in the doorway, one eye swollen, his nose bleeding. I tear my gaze to Jared who has a busted lip.

I pull the flannel from Jared's hands, and hop down from the unit. Walking over to Justin, taking his hand and guiding him to his bed.

"Lay down, baby. I need to clean you up." He's unsteady on his feet. I pat at the blood on his nose as the door slams and heavy footsteps hit the stairs.

"I'm going to get ice. Don't try to move, okay?"

When I get to the kitchen, Jared is bent into the freezer. Spanning from the nape of his neck to his lower back is a tattoo of a guitar. The detail is incredible. I recognize it immediately; it's my fender guitar that he and Justin bought me for my fourteenth birthday.

I loved that guitar until Jared left and I couldn't bear to play it again.

There are red nail marks across his shoulders and I blush at the damage I made.

"Ice," Jared shouts at me, tossing me a bag of ice. "So, you weren't welcoming me home then?"

"I'm sorry," I whisper, not knowing why I'm apologizing

"So am I, that you thought I was him. You really couldn't tell the difference between the way we both fuck?"

I flinch from his crass vocabulary. "Nice choice of words, Jared."

"Well, that's what we did, Beats. Sorry, does Justin make love to you?" He smirks, tipping a beer bottle to his lips and chugging.

"Fuck you."

He slams the bottle down and strides towards me, grabbing my hips and lifting me onto the sideboard. He brings a palm to each thigh and harshly opens my legs, crushing himself between them, his erection pushing against the juncture there.

"Fuck me? You sure, Beats? Because you know it's me this

time. Does he fuck you hard like that? Does he make you scream?"

I bring my palm down across his cheek, the contact ringing out into the room. He doesn't even flinch.

"Mmm, I like it rough, baby." He drops his tone low and breathes against my ear. "Just like you do."

My nipples tighten and my core begs for more.

"Does Justin give it to you rough like you need it, Beats?" I feel his smirk on my cheek.

I push at his shoulders. "You son of a bitch! Tonight was meant to be him! Our first time together! You took that from him, from us, like you took my fucking heart when you abandoned us! It took me forever to open myself up again and you come back and wreck me all over again!"

My words make him flinch. Pain blazes across his eyes but he recovers quickly.

"From what I heard you opened yourself up for all the football team, Beats. My poor brother the last one on your list to make it a full team?"

I feel like someone has invaded his body. "What are you talking about?"

He scoffs at me, moving away and leaning against the opposite counter. "I kept tabs. I needed to keep tabs on…Justin, so I kept in contact with someone here. They told me all about how you turned into the town whore. Sorry, I mean mini whore since your Mom already has that title."

Ice washes through me. Who is this person I let into my body?

"How can you say that to me?" I slide to my feet and walk until I'm almost touching him. Looking into his eyes at the conflicted emotions. "I loved you more than life. You were air for me, Rift, and when you left it was like living in darkness. My sun was gone. You made me feel like summer lived in my veins when we were together, so when you took off without a goodbye, a harsh winter set up shop within me, leaving me hurt, bitter and cold. It took two years before I let myself love Justin and he was supposed to be my first. I don't know who gives you your information but it's way off."

I turn to walk away but he grabs me around the upper arm, spinning me around to face him. "Your first, Beats? Your first what?"

I watch as understanding settles in his features.

"Did I just take your virginity hard against a wall?" His voice breaks, the torment sparks in his eyes. I yank my arm free and walk away. I reach for the ice melting in the bag from the counter and make my way up to Justin.

He's sleeping. Wrapping the ice in a towel, I hold it over his eye and he stirs, smiling up at me. "Hey, Meds. I'm so sorry. I should have told you so you weren't blindsided like that, but he isn't staying and neither are we. He's not the same person who left." Panic fills his voice; he's trying to convince me but he doesn't need to. I already know he's not my Rift, and now I'm left to deal with the guilt crawling in my skin like poison polluting my damaged soul. "Why didn't you tell me about Josie?" A sob tears from his chest and breaks my heart further "I only found out last night, it didn't seem real. I don't know what I'm meant to feel." Bringing his hand up to cover his face so I can't see his tears he sobs. Tears burst from my eyes without permission, his pain coating me in its grief. I lay with him and we cry until we fall asleep.

Justin

Guilt, it can be just as painful as sorrow,
It can eat away at you like death
It can taint memories, taint your heart, and taint your soul
Play with your mind making the person that is you harder to
find
Making you unable to give, unable to live

Heartbreak is worse than death, it cripples the soul
Tortures your being, questions your beliefs
Changes the way you think, act, or breathe
It introduces you to the darkness in the world
The darkness buried in you
It prevents reasoning, prevents you being you,
Making you unable to give, unable to live

Love can bring warmth to the body, light to the soul, a beat to
the heart
Love can bring you light in the darkness
Peace to your mind, reasoning to your troubles
A sleeve to your tears
It can be the sun in the winter, the thaw in the ice, turn bad to
nice

If you let yourself breathe, feel. Give... live

Who are you to me? What will it be?

"WHAT ARE YOU reading?" Jared asks me.

I hand him the brown leather pad. "It's Meadow's. She's writing again."

"What do you mean again?"

I pin him with a glare. "She stopped writing when you left. She stopped playing."

Sorrowful emotions dance across his face but I'm too mad at him to care if he's hurting right now. When Dad told me he called, and that our Mom had died, my emotions were jumbled. I was happy Jared was alive and well, and sad that he'd waited for bad news before getting in contact. I felt grief for my Mom, an ache from memories of my childhood that assaulted me and replayed all the happy moments we had as a family every time my mind would repeat the words *she's dead*. She was never coming back. We were never close and she didn't even look my way when she left but I loved her. It's a weird feeling that I can't quite get a handle on. I seem to jump from one emotion to the next like a yo yo. And then sitting there in the shadow of my mind I had the fear Jared was back and I couldn't keep him from Meadow.

I know she loves me and she's angry with Jared but I also know how intense their love was. That's what I struggled with the most when he left. Not how he could so easily leave me, even though we shared everything, but how he could leave Meadow. The sun rose and set with her where he was concerned. I could never leave her and I'm terrified he will take her from me.

"I had my reasons for leaving," I hear him mutter.

Ignoring him I stand when the shower turns off. I grab the book from him and place it back on top of Meadow's bag.

It's been seven days since Jared came home and to say things have been strained would be an understatement. Jared wasn't meant to stick around after Mom was buried but he told me he's hanging around for a few more days. I won't leave Meadow's side. I know I'm being needy, insecure and blatantly obvious but I just can't shake the fear of her leaving me. Jared is to blame for my anxiety; he made me this weak person when he left with Mom. It changed me, made me realize that at any given time your life can change, and people you love leave.

"Hey." Meadow pulls me from my thoughts. She's standing in her workout gear, her hair pulled tight into a ponytail. She's dropped weight this week, and I can already see the change in her body.

"I know I just showered but I think I'm going to hit the gym for a while. I need to get rid of some energy before I can go to sleep." A smile tilts her lips but it doesn't reach her eyes.

"I'll take you, I'm heading that way," Jared offers.

"No, I'll take her," I interject.

Her sad eyes drift between us. "I'm actually going to jog there."

"That's dangerous. It's late, Beats. I'll jog with you."

My stomach is in knots. "I'll jog with her," I all but growl at him.

"Guys, seriously. I'll be fine." She turns on her heel and leaves the room.

"What the fuck is your problem, Justin? You can't stop me from spending time with her."

The fear creeps in, wrapping its hands around my throat. "I won't let you take her from me. You left her, left *us*. I love her. I can't let you take her from me."

I feel the heat from his body on the back of me. He's breathing heavy near my ear.

"You sound like a psycho, Justin. Stop being such a fucking pussy."

His words cut deep because I feel like a freak but it was him who made me this way.

"Fuck you, Jared."

I hurry out of the room and down the stairs. Meadow is just opening the front door. "Meds, wait. I'll come with you. I don't want you jogging in the dark on your own."

She turns to me with a smile. "You're overprotective, But okay."

Relief settles inside me. She's still mine, and now it's just about waiting for Jared's departure.

Justin

A WHOLE SEVEN more days have passed and things haven't got any better. We put off moving early to start our college life until things are more settled. Jared and I have constantly been at each other's throats. Dad stayed away which gave Meadow one less thing to worry about; she still worries about what he thinks of her, and even though he tried to talk me into dumping her when we first got together, he hasn't brought her up since. He seems to accept us and never makes me feel awkward having her here.

I just wish she would come around and make more effort with him. Apart from Uncle Drew, my Dad is my only family that's stays around and he means the world to me. He has always supported me and encouraged my football, and I plan on putting a ring on Meadow's finger so they will have to learn to get along.

"Hey, I'm back," I call out. I had a leaving dinner with the coach and the guys on the team. I left early because I didn't want to leave Meadow here with Jared, that's how insecure I've let myself become. It angers me that I'm being weak and un-trusting of Meadow; she has given me no reason to worry, but I do anyway.

I hear voices coming from upstairs so I mount them two at a time and enter my room. Meadow is standing in the bathroom doorway, my Dad is a few feet in front of her, and she's crying and covering her bare chest.

"What the fuck's going on?"

Her body is shaking. I go to her, and she clings to me, gripping my t-shirt so hard her nails scrap the skin underneath.

"What the fuck happened?" I bellow to my Father.

"I caught her with your brother, throwing herself all over him. He bailed when I told him I would tell you."

My worst fear just spilled from my Father's lips.

"No, no," Meadow whimpers next to me. I turn to her, slipping my shirt off and over her.

"Where is Jared, Med?" fear, pain, *guilt* fill her eyes. My heart drains of blood. She's shaking her head. "He did leave bu…"

I push her back. I feel sick, and the room feels too small, the walls closing in on me.

"She's been playing you both for years, Justin. She's just like her mother."

His words slice at me like a knife.

"It didn't… it wasn't… Your Dad, he hates me, he did this," she stutters.

My anger flares, erupting from the pent up anxiety of the past weeks. "Don't try to blame him, Meadow. Have you been fucking around with my brother after everything? After he left you and I had to pick up the pieces? I should have listened to him and left you where you belonged, with your mother."

Her body quakes as tears stain her cheeks. I feel like I'm dying. She reaches for me but I step back.

"Get out!"

Her sobs torch the air, thickening the inferno flaring out of control inside me. She rushes from the room and I hear the front door slam behind her. Disintegrating my heart.

MEADOW

I AVOIDED ANY interaction with Jared. It was difficult because he was determined to talk to me. He stared at me over dinner, making it impossible to eat. He watched every move I made and so did Justin; it was so hard to be around them both. Can you love two people at once? Can you need love from two people? Can you ever move on from your first love?

The more time Jared spent at the house, the more Rift I could see in him. He was still passionate, funny, intense, dedicated to music. But he was also different. He was tougher, he had a harder edge then he used to. He seemed way older than his years, like he had grown up much sooner than the rest of us. He had life experience. I so wanted to know where he had been. What he had been doing all this time. But I was too afraid to speak to him in front of Justin.

*

It's been two weeks since Jared got back and tonight is the first time we've been alone.

He wastes no time cornering me in Justin's room.

"You can't avoid me forever, Beats. I'm not leaving until we have this talk."

He's so close I can smell his body wash. God, he smells good. Memories of us flood my mind and I look over to the wall where he took me. He follows my gaze and steps closer. "What are you thinking about, Beats?"

His voice drips with seduction, my heart rate accelerates.

"Nothing," I whisper.

"That's a lie and you know it. I can make that memory more vivid for you if you like?" He's so close his breath is burning my skin.

"Back off, Jared. Don't you care about Justin?" I try to appeal to the brother side of him because I'm so weak I don't know if I can tell him no if he pushes me any further.

He steps back. "He took what was mine." He sounds so deadly serious my eyebrows pinch together.

"You left me. You left me in a heap on my mother's floor, Jared. I would have never made it without Justin. He made me breathe again." The pain is back in his eyes, but I keep going. "You didn't even give me a chance to explain."

"What was there to explain? You knew Dad was fucking around with your mother and you kept it from me. My Mom was a mess. He beat her, did you know that? He would do it in places that wouldn't show. He told her he was fucking your Mom, he tortured her with details, sent her into a depression so bad that she was practically comatose for ages. He threatened her to keep her quiet."

Warm salty wetness seeps onto my lips. I'm crying and I hadn't even noticed.

"I had to get her away, Beats. She told me she had been following your Mom; she wanted to see what that woman had that she didn't."

"You could have talked to me. You destroyed me when you left."

"I was so mad at you, and then my Mom talked about how much your Mom had ruined her, and it made me angrier with you for keeping it a secret, for lying to me. As time passed I tried to convince myself we were young and it was a puppy love we could move on from, but I couldn't move on. Thoughts of you consumed me. Memories of us were what kept me sane while I tried to look after Mom.

I was planning on getting settled down and coming to talk to you. It had been four months, and I decided to charge my old phone and found texts from Melissa, telling me you'd moved on. I phoned her and she told me you were dating Logan from the football team. She said you were rebelling, going from one player to the next. I didn't believe her so I drove into town and there you were at a game, wearing preppy clothes, cheering for Logan and it broke my fucking heart. I didn't want to believe it Beats, but my Dad and his hateful words echoed in my mind along with my Mom's and I just…"

His hands are on my shoulders, his face contorted into a painful expression.

"She was lying, Jared. I changed the way I dressed because I needed to strip away what reminded me of you, but I've never even spoken to Logan, you asshole. I went to the games for Justin, if I was cheering it would have been for him and only so I seemed normal and not the walking corpse I had been since the day you KILLED ME" I scream. How dare he believe I would go from him to anyone and everyone? "She played you to hurt me. She's always hated me. And you let her, how could you ever think that of me?" I shake my head already knowing the answer. No matter how much I try to not be her, everyone will always cast me with the same title as my mother.

His hands slide to my neck. "I still love you, Beats. I know it's bad for Justin but I can't help it. We belong together, you know we do."

"I can't do that to him. When you left, it changed him. He had panic attacks if I didn't answer my phone. If he couldn't find me, he would freak out and have everyone looking for me. He was so scared I'd up and leave him to go find you. It took him so long to get over it and now I see him like it again, I couldn't leave him. You thought so shitty of me too Jared. You will always see my mother in me."

The lines on his face disappear as the cold Jared takes Rift's place.

"Fine, well tell my brother goodbye for me. And just know I

don't see anyone in you but you, Beats. I may have let anger and people influence my mind but never my heart. You live there, you're its beat, always were and always will be."

I grab his shirt. "Wait, you can't leave."

I know I can't have them both but the dread and sorrow my soul feels of the thought of him leaving us again is too intense. I can't let him walk away from us again it hurts to much.

"You can't have us both, and I won't survive seeing you with him. I love him he's my brother but I love you more. I'd end up killing him."

He tugs free. Grabbing his bag from the floor, he walks to the bedroom door as his Dad walks in. "What's going on?"

"Nothing. I'm leaving,"

"Rift, please don't," I cry out but he doesn't stop. I hear his chunky boots carry him down the stairs and out the front door.

I'm left staring into the cold, hateful eyes of Mr Jacobs. My insides weaken, and I walk slowly to the bathroom, hoping to get in there and lock myself in until Justin gets home. I only make it to the doorway before he grabs the back of my neck and throws me forward with such force I slide across the cold tiled floor.

I've always complained to Justin and Jared about how cold and clinical this bathroom looks; it's all white, no splash of color anywhere and it has now become a white padded cell holding me hostage. Mr Jacobs' heavy body comes down on me. He's holding my hair; the smell of alcohol stings my nose as his harsh words spill all over me. "You're nothing but a fucking whore, playing both my boys just like your mother did with me and my brother."

His painful grip pushes into my hip and he flips me onto my back and straddles my waist, pinning my arms either side of my head.

"Why do you hate me?" I sob. He words not making sense.

He leans forward and growls at me. "Because women like you ruin lives. You turn us into jealous messes. You use us for money, titles. You've been using my boys just like Mommy taught you to, using your beauty against us."

He reaches for the hem of my shirt and rips it open. My buttons fly across the bathroom, scattering with tiny taps as they land. He's exposed my bra for his greedy eyes. Sobs rack my body, making me shudder violently. The cold press of the tiles against my back keeps me grounded. I try to focus on any feeling but him. He tears the fabric clean from my skin. "Look at you. No wonder they can't get enough. Time to share with me, too."

"God, no please!" I beg choking on my cries. I've always known he was capable of this, that's why I've been so afraid of him. His mind has been raping me for years.

He flicks the front fastener to my bra, exposing my bare breasts, keeping my arms pinned with one hand. I squirm, trying to get free but he's too powerful. "Your body was made for sin, Meadow, just like your mother's."

I hear the front door open. Mr Jacobs' eyes widen. He jumps from my body, stumbling back into the bedroom as I scurry to my feet and cover my breasts. I hear footsteps coming towards me and pure relief floods my body as Justin enters the room. I move to the doorway, grabbing at him when he comes close enough.

"Get out!"

His words incinerate what's left of my heart leaving nothing but ashes.

MEADOW

"IT'S BEEN TWO months and you're already behind on classes, Meadow. You won't keep that scholarship if you don't even go to classes. You need to go see him and start college. You earned this scholarship."

I look into the brown eyes of my mother. "What has happened to you?" I ask, completely dumbfounded at the woman giving me advice. Actually seemingly bothered about my scholarship. I know she probably just wants me out of her hair once and for all.

I went away for two weeks after that night, and when I came back, Jared hadn't been back and no one knew where he went. Justin has left for Florida; he left letters for me with Drew but I can't read them, and I made Drew and my Mom swear to tell people I'm not staying here if anyone asks. I need to be invisible again and just blend into the scenery.

My classes started three weeks ago and my professors are only giving me two more days before they take me off their roster. Everything I worked for, making sure I could follow Justin to Florida state so he wouldn't be alone was all for nothing.

I'm used to the fear of being left alone; I am the poster child for a lonely childhood. My Father knocked my Mom up and left her as soon as the stick turned pink. Then her family abandoned us before I even took a breath. I had lots of 'uncles' come and go over the years. Mom thought that was a good term for her many boyfriends.

Then the most important person in my whole world left me, not once, but twice. I wonder how Justin is coping. Drew said he's struggling but he hurt me so bad. I'm struggling too and I don't know how to see him again but I know I have to.

I'VE BEEN STARING at the wooden door for at least twenty minutes, my heart pounding in my ears. I raise and lower my hand over and over but can't bring myself to wrap my knuckles on the door.

"Hey, can I help you?" I turn to see a blonde guy with brown eyes smirking at me. He points to the door I'm standing like a statue in front of. "This is my place."

I blink and realize what a freak I must seem. I clear my dry throat. "Oh, erm, sorry. I thought Justin Jacobs lived here."

The guy smiles and comes closer. "He does. I'm Max, his room-mate."

I return his smile. "Oh, right. I'm Meadow."

His eyes roam over me and his smile broadens. "Of course you are, I recognize you now." He laughs at my confusion and puts his key in the lock. "Justin has pictures of you."

My face flushes. "Oh, okay."

"I can see why he's so messed up over you. Are you blushing? That's cute" He winks. The flush travels further up my cheeks and down my neck. I shake my head and follow him over the threshold.

"I'm just playing trying to ease your tension, you been out there long?"

He raises his eyebrows knowingly. I try to smile but my lips refuse to tilt up. I shrug instead and look around the apartment I'm supposed to be living in with Justin, taking in the natural tones to the décor. The wide screen TV, and recliners scream guy pad. It's not until I notice all the pictures adorning the walls that it feels more homely.

"See." Max gestures to the pictures hanging from every wall. They're of me and Justin; the apartment is covered in them. "Drink?" He holds up a beer bottle and tilts it in my direction.

I look to my watch and scrunch my nose. "It's three o'clock in the afternoon."

This gains me a chesty laugh. "You're in college now, sweetheart. We're supposed to drink in the day."

"Where's Justin…" I don't get a chance to finish my sentence, the front door opens and groceries hit the floor with a thud.

"Meadow?" It comes out as question, like he's not sure if I'm actually standing here.

I nod. "Hey. I just wanted to see you so you don't get a shock if you see me on campus,"

The brown paper bag crumbles at his feet, groceries spilling out. He's frozen to the spot.

"Justin! Dude, you're freaking me out," Max says, walking over to pick up the contents of the bag.

"Meadow." He steps past Max and smashes his body to mine, holding so tight I struggle to breathe. "Where have you been? I've been out of my mind with worry."

I eventually get him to loosen his death grip. "I needed time." My voice comes out weaker then I meant it to, there's understanding in his eyes.

"I'm sorry, Med. I spoke to Jared. He called, and apparently he felt bad for leaving without saying goodbye." I hear the doubt in his voice. "He told me nothing happened between you, and then Dad admitted he was drinking and maybe you were just taking a shower and he jumped to conclusions."

He's smiling at me, happy with his Dad's answer for what happened. I can't even force a smile to grace my lips. My body stiffens at the mention of his Father, the memories from that night leaving cold shivers racing through me.

"Your Dad hates me and he is a liar," I grate out.

61

Justin sighs and rakes his hands through his hair. "He doesn't hate you, Med. He just doesn't want me making a mistake. He thinks I'm your stand-in for Jared."

Hearing him say that hurts for more reasons than one. First of all, I hate how he swallows whatever bullshit his Father feeds him. Second, I love him and he isn't a substitute for Jared. I love him on his own merit and never compare the two. But thirdly, after Jared left for the second time, It reminded me and magnified the hurt from the first time. I was so sick of feeling numb after he left, I needed Justin to take my hand and teach me exist again without him, give me a substitute for air so I could finally breathe again. I missed Justin and needed his presence for comfort, but I craved Jared. I miss him with every beat of my heart. So where does that leave things with Justin and me?

"Guys, I'm going to take off to give you some privacy." Max's voice comes from behind me. I had completely forgotten he was even there. We don't even acknowledge him as he walks out.

"Med, I can't argue with you about my Dad, I just can't. He's the only family I have. Please."

My body sags releasing the tension in my muscles, sighing I tell him. "I love you, Justin and because I do I will drop it."

The rigidity leaves his shoulders. "You love me still?" He sounds desperate, needy.

"I'll always love you. Before we were a couple, we were best friends. You have been a huge part of my life, don't ever question my love for you."

His huge exhale of breath tells me he's relieved. "I missed you so much. You can't do that to me, you can't leave me. We belong together, Meadow. You weren't meant for him, you were meant for me." He cups my face in both hands and descends his soft lips to mine for a few seconds before breaking away to swipe a stray strand of hair from my face. "I love you more. I'm supposed to be with you. I'll never leave you. I'll be your first and your last." Reaching for the hem of my sun dress, he whispers. "Let me be the first person to make love to you, and the last, Meds."

A lone tear falls from my eye as I struggle to look at him. I don't have to. Justin has known me since we were thirteen years old, we've been through everything together and he knows in this moment he won't be my first. My tear the only evidence he needs. He steps away from me, the material dropping from his fingertips.

"Look at me, Meadow."

I can't. One tear has turned into many, the gentle sobs forcing my body into a tremor.

"Oh, God. He was home for two fucking weeks. I never was your choice was I? Just a stand-in until you could have the right twin back." The pain in his voice cripples me. The guilt overwhelms my body. I crumble to the floor, my legs no longer steady enough to hold me. "I'll never forgive you for this," he whispers.

I look up at him through my tear-filled eyes; he looks disgusted. I've seen that look before in the hateful eyes of his Father.

"It's not like you think, Justin," I manage to strangle out.

"Did you or did you not fuck my brother?" He sounds so cold now, nothing like the boy who picked me up and mended my heart when his brother left it in tatters. "Answer the fucking QUESTION!" he roars, making me flinch.

"Yes, but…"

He doesn't give me a chance to finish. "Get out. I can't even look at you. You disgust me. You really are her daughter, Med, no matter how hard you tried not to be. Jared knew it too, that's why he left you again."

The realization of what I've lost crashes into me. The painful words from someone I've always loved and relied on blankets me with an icy chill. I feel like the first fall of winter's snow has fallen over my body, burying me. On the outside I will be perfect, like untouched snow, but underneath I will remain cold, my heart frozen, protected from the pain of the Jacobs twins.

I stand, feeling a little dizzy. I take a few deep breaths and without looking at him I leave.

Justin

I LIFT THE beer bottle to my lips, gulping it down like water.

"You need to chill with the drinking, we've only been here an hour and that's your fourth beer."

I look over at Max. "I'm nervous."

His throaty laugh makes me glare at him.

"Hey, less with the glaring. I'm doing you a favor. You sure she's even going to be here?"

I tip the beer bottle back to my lips, emptying the contents down my throat. I place the bottle on the table and hold my hand up to signal for Drew's new waitress to bring more drinks. Her flustered face fake smiles, with a nod in my direction. "She will be here, it's her Mom's wedding." I spin the coaster, needing to occupy my hands.

"From what you told me, she hated her Mom."

I look up at him. "It's still her Mom."

The barmaid makes it over to us, placing four bottles on the table. I look up at her to question the four and not two. "It saves me going back to the bar and you calling me straight back," she explains, annoyance evident in her tone. She turns on her heel and heads back to the bar.

I look over at Max. "Was it just me or was she being funny?"

Max laughs but then his smile falls from his lips. He lowers his bottle, taking in someone across the bar. I know it's Meadow; she elicits that reaction from men. "Damn," Max mutters.

I flick the coaster at his head; it rebounds off, hitting the bottles then the floor. I follow his gaze, and true enough, there she is in all her beautiful glory. I swallow, trying to clear the rush of saliva filling my mouth. She's wearing jean shorts, her long toned legs on display in wedged heel sandals with ribbons that travel up her calf. She's wearing a dark blue fitted t-shirt with *Monsters in the Dark* written across the chest. Her hair flows freely down her back.

"Justin. You going to be ok being around her, man. I don't know how you'll cope if she's still pissed" Max's voice snaps me from my thoughts.

"That's right, you don't know, but you know she's off limits so put your eyes back in your head and your dick back in your pants."

He raises his hands in mock surrender. "Chill. She's cute but I know she's off limits, not hurting for women here Just" He grins.

Truth is, I can't chill. It has been over a year since she walked out of my apartment and never came back. She was never on campus and it quickly became apparent that she had left for good.

I look back across the bar and find her unique violet eyes trained on me; there's so much in them, sorrow, guilt, love, memories. I return her look with the same intensity she's showing me. I lift my lips into a smile and her chest expand like she's releasing a breath. Her feet start to move in my direction and my heartbeat accelerates. Her flowery scent invades my space as she approaches.

"Hey," she murmurs.

"Hey, Meadow," Max says tilting his beer in her direction. Her eyes don't leave mine, even when she returns his greeting.

"You came," I say.

She looks around the bar and smiles. "I never thought I'd see the day. I just wanted to make sure it was true."

"Well, it is. So I guess were going to be family."

Her nose twitches and a tilt lifts her lips as she nods her head. "I don't think either of us has really ever had that." Pain tortures her still from the loneliness of never really having a real family and I still want to hold her take away her sorrow after all this time.

"Drink?" Max breaks the uncomfortable atmosphere that had fallen over us. Her face transforms into a beautiful grin.

"Hmm, I always liked you Max."

He chuckles as he slides out of the booth. "You called me Max. I didn't know if you would remember me."

She raises an eyebrow. "Are you kidding? You taught me I'm allowed to drink any time of the day. Some teachers stay with you." She places a hand over her heart and he beams down at her.

"Glad I had an effect on you." He winks and ushers her to the bar. I have to fight my instinct to not punch his face in, and try to remember she doesn't belong to me and this is just Max, who's like this with everyone.

I follow them to the bar.

"No way. Have you finished them already? I need to cut you off. You're going to die if you don't slow down."

Max and Meadow are both staring between me and the new barmaid; Ellie, I think she said her name was.

"Ellie, you need to learn if people are spending, you keep serving," I inform her.

She lifts a tea towel and begins wiping the bar. "Well, you haven't been paying so I'm not serving." She smirks.

I look at her in disbelief as Meadow begins to giggle. I cock an eyebrow and pin Meadow with a 'what's so funny?' stare.

"Ellie, serve my nephew his beer and serve my new daughter whatever she wants."

Ellie looks embarrassed, the tinge in her cheeks giving her away. "Sure, boss," she squeaks out. I can't help but smile. She places the drink in front of me, and before she can walk away I reach for her hand to hold her in place.

Her eyes dart to mine. "If you would have asked instead of jumping to conclusions I would have told you I don't need a beer. I have three on the table."

66

Her blush consume her face. A warm, soft hand touches my arm; I feel her touch all the way down to my groin.

"Don't be mean." Meadow's breasts unintentionally push against my arm and I'm back to being that thirteen-year-old boy who saw her cleavage for the first time when she stripped her sweater off and gave me my first of many erections.

I release my hold on Ellie and turn to Meadow. "How long you in town?"

"A week. You?"

"A week."

"Shots!" Max bellows, sliding shot glasses our way. We waste no time knocking them back. Meadow's Mom and Drew join us for a few drinks. Before we know it, they've disappeared upstairs and it's closing time.

"Let's go into town," Meadow slurs. She's completely letting her hair down, she seems to of changed quite a lot in the year away from us all.

Max raises a hand. "Yep, let's do it. I need a woman for the night."

"Okay, fine. But, Meds, you're not really dressed for the club."

She looks down at herself. Mine and Max's eyes follow her observation of her body.

"She looks fucking hot," Max says. I glare at him.

"I look more ready for the beach than the club, don't I?" she moans. "Oh, hang on." She opens the hatch and disappears behind the bar. I hear her rustling around, then clothes appear on the bar. "My suitcase." She beams.

I look over the bar and down at her feet is her suitcase.

"I came straight here, I haven't checked into my hotel yet." She smiles then falters. "Oh, shit. I haven't checked in yet!"

I laugh at her panicked expression. "It's fine, you can check in anytime," I reassure her, and her smile reappears.

"Ok" She comes back around the bar and holds up a red piece of material. "This okay?"

"Fuck yes!" Max says.

My mouth has gone dry.

"Okay, turn around you two." We both turn towards the bar like whipped school boys. I watch in the mirror that spans the entire length of the bar as Meadow lifts her top from her body. Her black lacy bra hugs her perfect tits, her skin is flawless, a golden tone of smooth silk. I shift to accommodate my growing erection and watch as her fingers fumble with the buttons on her shorts. She manages to unzip them, shimmying them down her thighs. Her little black panties cling to her like leather to skin on a hot day; she's pin-up worthy.

"Oh my God, I need to get laid," Max groans next to me, and it's then I realize I'm not the only one getting a show. She slips her dress over her head.

"Done, you can turn arou…damn! You can see me in the mirror! Justin!"

I have to laugh; she's so cute when she's drunk. I haven't seen her this carefree since before Jared left the first time.

"You told us to face away, Med. We did as we were told." I try to keep a straight face.

"For what it's worth, Meadow, I think you should lose the dress and just come clubbing in your underwear," Max informs her.

She pouts. "You don't like my dress?"

Max looks at me and then back to her and we all break into a laugh. "Should we tell Drew we're leaving? He might need to lock up?" she asks.

I shake my head and lead her outside.

MEADOW

LAST NIGHT'S EVENTS keep replaying in my mind as I'm waking up. My memory's foggy, and then completely blank after Max asked Justin if Jared was coming to the wedding and Justin said, *"No, he's settled down with a girl. He has no reason to come back, there's nothing he wants here."*

That hurt and that was what led me to drink multi-colored cocktails at Club Ruby. The ice I had formed the day I walked out on Justin, evaporated into a puddle when I saw him. It had served me well, never allowing any man to chip away at it. I was the ice princess and happy to wear that title until every pep talk I had given myself before coming back blew away on the wind of the tornado that was the Jacob twins. I was back to being the girl completely consumed by the need to love them. Justin was comfort, my body automatically soothed when he spoke to me. I vaguely remember Max dry humping some girl in the corner of the bar, and Justin and I giggling about it like we were in high school. I remember Justin asking me why I was so happy and free. I told him it's because I refuse to love again and it's freeing. It wasn't exactly true. I just refused to love anyone new.

I moan, strangely aroused. My mind comes more into consciousness, telling me there's a hand between my thighs. I react on instinct, and my hand goes down on top of the hand that's down there to still the movement. My body stiffens. I slowly peel open one eye, and staring back at me is the golden glow of Justin's eyes.

"Hey beautiful," he says, kissing my neck. A million questions race through my mind: *'Why is Justin kissing me like we've never been apart?'*

'How the fuck did I end up here?'

'Where is here?'

'Why am I naked?'

'Oh, God. Did we finally have sex and I missed it in a drunken stupor?'

"I want to hear you moan again before we have to leave this room," Justin says into my neck. So the answer is yes; I clearly blacked out sex with Justin. God, my life sucks. I can't believe I put out so easily, and to Justin! We haven't even talked about the way we left things.

The phone rings and saves me from having to decide whether to bolt or let him touch me. Pulling away from me he lifts the receiver. "Okay, thanks." He puts the phone down and hurries from the bed, gathering our clothes as he does.

I sit up, pulling the sheet up to cover me. My mouth is dry and there's a slight burn in my throat. "Who was that?" I ask hoarsely.

Justin starts hopping on one foot, trying to put his sock onto other. "My wakeup call. Med, listen I need to run, but I want to talk about what happened. Can I meet you later?"

Brushing a hand through the tangled mess on top of my head I mutter, "Yeah, sure."

"Where are we?" I ask, looking around the room. There are dark blue drapes pulled across the entire back wall, and a vanity unit with a large mirror above. The carpets are dark blue like the drapes, and the bedding is crisp white.

"My suite. It's rented for the week."

"Yo, Justin, someone's at the door!" Max calls.

Panic crosses his face as he pulls on his jeans and t-shirt. His eyes are looking everywhere but at me.

"Why are you freaking out?"

"I'm not. Just stay in here, Meds." He rushes to the door and exits, closing it behind him. Sliding from the bed I stumble over to the vanity mirror and groan at the woman looking back at me. My hair looks like I stepped out of the eighties and my eyes are rimmed with black makeup. I pull myself away from my self-loathing when I hear muffled voices coming from outside the door. I move closer, pinning my ear against it. My heart begins to pound against my rib cage. I swing open the door to find Max's naked back in my view, blocking the doorway like a security guard. He turns and slings an arm over my shoulders. I try to shake him off but he gives me a pleading stare. I look over to see Justin holding someone. When he releases her, she turns to me. "Oh, I didn't realize you had a guest, Max." There's no warmth in her tone.

"Yeah, this is Meadow, she's the bride's daughter," Max says. "We went out last night."

Her eyes travel up my body and her lips turn up in judgment. "How welcoming of her."

She screams sorority in her knee-length skirt, blouse, and sweater resting over her shoulder. Her blonde hair is poker straight with a side bang, and she has pearls around her neck.

"Well, baby, if he's going to be bringing just anyone here all week, I want a separate suite," she says while rubbing Justin's arm. He looks over at me, guilt evident in his face. I'm about to go hide in the room but my feet falter and my heart rattles against my chest as a tremor ricochets through me.

"I needed that. I shouldn't have had so much to drink and then driven for three hours," Jared says as he walks into the room, buttoning his fly. He looks up with a smile but it drops when he sees me standing in nothing but a sheet with Max's arm around my shoulders. His eyes flare with rage, a sheen coating them, lighting the amber glow like someone blowing on a naked flame. He takes in a nearly nude Max in a slow observation, starting at his toes and traveling the length of his body to his extended arm. Max must see it too, must feel the wave of hostility rolling over us like the sea crashing against rocks. He quickly removes his hand.

"What the fuck is this?" he asks into the room, not aimed at anyone in particular.

Justin's head drops.

"I'm going to get dressed," Max tells us, creeping across the living room and disappearing through a door.

"Maria, would you mind going downstairs and getting us a table for breakfast? I need to talk to my brother," Justin says. She nods, giving me another disapproving sneer before she kisses his cheek and leaves.

"What the hell is she doing here with some douche?" Jared asks.

"She isn't here with him, she's here with me," Justin informs him all too happily.

A smirk lifts Jared's lips. "I take it Miss Stepford doesn't know, hence the douche standing in for you. Or was he part of the party?"

"Don't be disgusting, Jared. What are you even doing here?" I ask.

"Med, why don't you go put some clothes on?" Justin suggests.

Jared's laugh sends chills through me. "Why? She hasn't got anything we haven't both seen, Justin." He walks closer to me. "I'm here for my uncle's wedding. Justin said for me to come stay with him for the week to catch up being as he was here too. Guess you've both done some catching up, huh?"

I can't tear my eyes from him. He's wearing low rise jeans, a wife beater vest, a black leather jacket, and shit kicker boots; he is sex personified and I feel myself dampen between my thighs with every step he takes towards me.

"You're looking good, Beats." His eyes drop to my nipples tenting the sheet. A blush heats my cheeks as a knowing smile plays on his lips.

"Meadow." I flinch at the tone of Justin's voice. I look over Jared's shoulder to see Justin's glare narrowed on us. "Go put some clothes on. Jared, stop fucking looking at her like that."

His laugh makes me jump. "Still paranoid she wants me and not you? I thought you moved on with Stepford? Besides, I think she likes me looking at her, judging by that flush on her skin. Are you pink all over, Beats?"

Justin storms across the room, grabbing me by the wrist. "For fuck's sake, Jared! She's standing there covered in my scent and you're still making a play for her?"

I can't breathe. This isn't happening, how can I be so stupid? And just let the past go so easily. I feel sick when Jared's face falls and pain flitters across his golden eyes. It doesn't last, his cold façade slips quickly into place. "Hey, I'm used to sharing, Justin. You always wanted my stuff." His grin bores into me as Justin's grip tightens on my wrist. The tension clogs the air like smoke in an inferno, their eyes blazing into each other's.

"For God's sake!" I scream, pulling the sheet from my body and holding my hands up. "Why not share me? Come on, sandwich me together like the piece of meat you think I am! I'm sick of this shit. You can both go to hell."

Both pairs of eyes are on my exposed flesh, raking over my naked form like they've never seen the female anatomy before.

"Shit…I…err..!" Max chokes out. The warmth drains from me.

Justin reaches for the sheet and holds it in front of me while Jared shoves me backwards into the room I vacated. "Turn around if you like your teeth!" he bellows at Max.

I stumble back into Justin's room and slip my dress over my head, finding my panties and sliding them up my legs. Jared's face sets into a grimace as he looks between me and the sex-rumpled bed.

"She can get dressed on her own."

"Do one, Justin. Haven't you got a breakfast to get to?"

Justin rubs his hands down his face. My fury boils and I poke him in the chest.

"You have some explaining to do, Justin. Who's the blonde?"

Jared sniggers. I turn my glare to him but he just smirks at me, a glint in his panty-dropper eyes. He still has power over me and my body. "He didn't tell you he had a girlfriend, huh? That's low, Justin."

"I'm sorry, Meds. Yes, she's my girlfriend."

I hear an unnatural laugh rip from my chest, throwing my hands up, then letting them collapse at my side. "Did you know Jared was coming? Because you made it quite clear he wouldn't be here and that it was him who was settled with a girlfriend."

Jared's growl sounds primal. "You liar! Is that what you had to do to get in her panties?"

The front door opens and closes. Within seconds, the blonde appears in the doorway of Justin's bedroom. "Justin, what's going on? I waited."

"Not long enough!" he snaps. Flinching from his abrupt reply she storms from the room. "Shit, wait. Maria!" he calls after her and I'm left standing in in last night's clothes with Jared staring at me.

"Now you can finally compare the two of us, huh, Beats?"

A tear leaks from my eye without permission. He closes the distance between us and swipes across my cheek to capture the tear with the pad of his thumb, bringing it to his lips and sucking the dampness from it.

"I've never compared you, and I was so wasted last night I don't even remember it. None of it even matters anyway. I should never have come back here, and as soon as my Mom's wedding is over, I'm leaving and I won't ever come back again."

I push past him and head through the lounge area where Max is sitting on the couch. I brush past Justin who's whispering something to this Maria girl. I ignore him when he calls my name, opening the door and slamming it behind me. I rush down the hall to escape my past heartache that has a way of becoming a fresh wound every time I see Jared. I ignore the judgemental eyes of the other guests. I feel so disgusted with myself for doing the walk of shame. For not remembering the night before and for my traitorous body for disobeying me when I tell it we no longer love, lust or care for Rift. I know what people are thinking and they're right; the walk of shame really *is* shameful.

"Meadow, you left your bag and shoes." Max runs towards me, sympathy in his eyes, which only makes me feel worse.

"Thanks." I take my belongings from him.

"I'm sorry about what happened. It seems like a really tense situation and Justin's brother is all kinds of scary."

I nod and offer a weak smile. "Why didn't you tell me Justin had a girlfriend?"

"I didn't know anything was going to happen with you two, and you left the club before me so I didn't know he brought you home. But as sweet as you are and as much as I like you, my loyalty is with Justin and he asked me to keep his personal business quiet." He rubs my arm and looks genuinely sorry but I don't care. He played me just like Justin did and I feel sick to my stomach. I turn from him and hit the elevator button. It opens straight away and I send up a silent thank you.

I rush inside and repeatedly hit the lobby button as Jared and Justin come barrelling out from the hotel room and head down the hall towards me. The doors close before they reach me.

As the elevator descends, my stomach rolls and my heart goes with it. There's a loud ding before the doors slide open; the foyer is bustling with people and I feel like a cheap whore in my rumpled dress.

I hang my head and make my way to the service desk, pulling out my credit card and handing it over to the desk clerk who's grinning at me like he knows all my secrets. "Can I help you, Ma'am?" The smile never leaves his face; he looks like he's starring in a tooth paste commercial. I can't take any more people judging me, I can't walk into another hotel looking like this so I need a room here and need to get inside it as soon as possible.

"Can I book a room for the night, please?" He taps away on his computer and swipes my credit card. I wince as he does, knowing I'm blowing way too much of my limit to book a room here, but I need a shower and some alone time to refocus.

My hotel room looks like the bedroom from Justin's suite. I strip my dress and panties off and head straight to the shower, letting the heat and steam rinse away the harsh reality of being back here with the Jacobs twins.

"MOM, PLEASE JUST bring my suitcase. I need clean clothes. I have nothing to put on and I can't wear last night's dress"

"You know how busy I am. I'm getting married in three days, Meadow."

"I know, and if you bring me clothes I can help."

"I'll send Ellie."

"Fine."

I put the phone down with a sigh.

I knew I should never have come back here. My Mom cried and begged me to come, and if it wasn't for Drew phoning me later that day to ask me, I wouldn't have let her fake tears draw me in.

By four o' clock Ellie still hasn't shown up and I'm left sitting here in a hotel robe I found on the back of the bathroom door.

A knock on the door comes as my stomach growls, letting me know I waited too long before ordering room service. I pull the door open and immediately close it when I realize I was wrong about it being room service.

"Beats, open the door. I have your suitcase."

Damn it, I need my clothes, why does he have it. "Leave it outside and go away, Jared."

"Maybe I'll open it and take me a souvenir."

I throw the door open to find him laughing, arms folded over his impressive chest with his stupid, sexy messy hair falling over his stupid weird-colored eyes, wearing those stupid, sexy jeans. Grrr.

"You have murder in those eyes, Beats."

I give him a sarcastic grin. "Don't be silly, I'm thrilled to have you here tormenting me."

He laughs and it penetrates right to my core, making me squeeze my thighs together. "Mmm, now there's something completely different in those eyes, Beats."

I roll my eyes and reach for my suitcase. He grabs my wrist. "I'll bring it in."

"No Rift, I don't want you in here, how did you even get my case?"

"I went to the bar looking for you I wanted to apologize for this morning, I was a dick" Sighing he swipes a hand through his hair. "It was a shock and as you know I'm not good dealing with the whole you and Justin shit" I nod my head

"Ok, fine" reaching for my suitcase he again stops me.

I huff like a child and stomp back inside the room. He sniggers, following me. "I don't want to argue with you. Can't we just spend some time together? Watch a movie?"

"A movie? Really? You expect me to believe that's what you want?"

He grasps my shoulders. "I just want to watch a movie, and spend time with you without there being tension. For old time's sake. Do this for me." The knock at the door makes him scowl.

I prod his chest with my finger. "Room service, calm down. Your acting like a jealous boyfriend Jared, don't make me remind you how long it's been since that's what we were. Can you get that while I go get dressed?"

He grins and looks down at my dressing gown. "Don't get dressed on my account." I slap his chest and point to the door.

I open the bathroom door to find Jared laid out across the bed, my burger half eaten in his hand. "I left you the chips and the pickle from the burger. I can't believe you stay at a fancy ass hotel and order burger and fries, Beats,"

"Hey, this hotel wasn't my choice and I'll probably have to starve for a month to pay off the dent it will leave in my credit card.

And for your information nowhere is too fancy for burger and fries. It's all the food groups in one."

"I must admit, it was a good burger." I smile at how easy things are when we're just two friends sharing a meal. "So, what film, Beats? Tell me you still love action flicks. I can't watch that Ryan Gosling bullshit."

I fake a shocked face. "Actually, he stars in my favorite movie."

He grimaces. "Shit, what happened to you? You really are one of the girls now. I can't watch that Notebook film again."

I let out a full belly laugh, hunching over and holding my stomach. Once I regain my composure, I swipe at the tears trailing down my cheeks. "I can't imagine you ever watching *The Notebook*."

He grins and it's beautiful. "I watched it with Mom."

My smile falls and so does his. We stare at each other for a few minutes, and then he breaks the silence. "I'll watch it if that's your favorite movie."

My smile returns. "Actually I was referring to one of his many other movies." I raise a mocking brow at him for assuming it would be *The Notebook*. "*Drive*, have you seen it?"

"The one where he's the getaway stunt driver that kicks mobster ass in the end?" he asks. I smile and nod. "What's your favorite part?" He smirks like he thinks I'm lying.

I shift so I'm propped up next to him on some pillows and I sprinkle salt on my fries. "Promise not to laugh?" He nods, the sexy smirk still in place. "Okay. It's when he's driving the getaway car, the jet black Ford Mustang. The purr of the engine as it begins to accelerate, getting faster and faster until the engine's roaring. It just gets me the same way Jared Leto's voice does, you know? Builds from a purr into a panty- wetting roar." I pop a fry into my mouth and sneak a look at him. His mouth is open and his eyes are smouldering.

"That's the sexiest thing I've ever heard."

I laugh and shake my head. "It's the truth. So, you want to watch it?"

"I don't know if I can now, knowing your panties are getting wet during that scene. I'm hard just thinking about it. Knowing it's happening a foot away will drive me fucking crazy."

I choke on my fry. "Jesus, Jared!"

"Let's see what's on their pay per view instead." He gets off the bed and slides the cabinet door open, revealing a flat screen TV and coffee making facilities. He flicks the remote and the TV comes to life. "How about a Die Hard marathon?"

I look at the clock. "Haven't you got anywhere to be?"

He smiles and throws himself back on the bed. "Nope."

I FEEL HER warm body curled up next to mine. Her scent is intoxicating, filling my senses and driving my cock into overload. She's so beautiful, funny, loving and I've missed her so much.

I keep getting flashes of seeing her naked after spending the night with Justin and it's eating away at me, but not enough to stay away from her. I can't believe he told her I wasn't coming here after he asked me to. I knew I shouldn't have left him my number, I should have just taken off, cutting everyone off like last time. The fact he was so willing to stay with the woman-beating prick instead of leaving with me and Mom still tears me up inside.

Seeing them both looking their ages, enjoying being young in college makes me realize how different my last few years were to theirs. I had to find a place to live, drop out of school and find work. Mom quickly spiralled further into depression and if it wasn't for meeting my now brother and best friend Razor, in a bar one night, I wouldn't have survived. He gave me a new family, money, a home and introduced me into a new life.

So why do I always end up back here, hurting over this woman, her always picking Justin over me?

God, I've tried everything to get over her. Fighting her out, drinking her out, and fucking her out. Nothing works. That girl is in every cell of my body and only a body bag will release me from her thrall. Even then, I think my ghost will haunt her.

Her ass shifts back into my groin, pulling my focus into the now, and fuck, I can't help but grind forward. I hear her sharp intake of breath and then feel the cold emptiness as she jumps from the bed.

"Shit, we fell asleep together."

I can't help but laugh. "We're grownups, Beats. We can spend the night together if we want to."

She grimaces. "I know, it's just... I feel slutty."

"Why? We didn't do anything."

She nods, running her hand through her hair then begins pacing up and down.

"I know. It just doesn't look good, me spending the night with Justin then you."

"Nothing happened, and who's going to know anyway?"

She smiles. "You're right. I don't know why I care. Justin really screwed me over."

I slip off the bed and go to where she's pacing. I reach for her shoulders to stop her. "He's fucking crazy bringing that robot type woman here when he had the chance to be with you. Don't let him see how much he got to you."

Her lips lift and my heart skips a beat. How can I still love her like this, after so long without her?

"Let's go get breakfast," I say, trying to stop myself from leaning in to claim her lips.

"I need to shower and change."

"Okay, well I'll go back to my room to shower and change then I'll pick you up after."

"Sounds like a plan."

When I get back to the suite, Justin immediately gets in my face.

"Where the hell have you been?"

I push him away. "What's it got to do with you?"

His chest touches mine as he steps into me. "I know you were with her. Drew said you took off with her suitcase."

My temper begins to blaze, a slow hum pumping through my veins. My mind raging war with the man in me against the brother. He took what was mine, If he was anyone else he wouldn't be walking or talking right now. "Where's your girlfriend, Justin? You know, the one you forgot to mention before bedding Beats. You should be worried if I took off with her, not Beats. She's none of your business."

His face turns in a snarl. "You son of a bitch, Jared. You fucking son of a bitch. How many times are we going to do this same routine?"

I shove him hard in the chest. "For as long as you continue to take things that aren't yours."

"She's more mine than she is yours. You left her when we were kids. You had puppy love, nothing more. What we had was real!"

"Well, it didn't feel like puppy love when I was buried deep in her pussy, Justin."

His jaw tics and his fists fly towards me. I let him make contact; my tooth pierces my lip. I smile as blood trickles down my chin. He hits like a bitch ...still. Max rushes over from the couch and grips Justin from behind. "God, you two! She's not an object to fight over."

I throw him a glare as Justin shrugs him off.

"Mind your business"

"You two are crazy. I'm going for lunch. You better get your shit together before Maria, gets back from the salon."

I push past Justin and head down the hall to my room but he's quick on my heels. "Where is she? I need to talk to her, explain."

Anger boils in my veins, drowning me in rage. Turning, I pin him against the wall by his throat. "You fucking lied to her! You made her think I wasn't coming here because I have a girl, just so you could make a play for her. What do you think's going to happen with you two? You have Miss Stepford."

His hands pull at my wrists, having no effect on the grip I have him in. "Her name is Maria George. Stop being a dick."

"That's all you have to say?"

"I don't need to tell you shit about me and Meadow. You have no idea how we feel about each other."

I pull him forward then slam him back. His head cracks against the wall, making him wince from the impact. I release my hold. "You're crazier than I thought," I go to my room and close the door.

Once I'm showered and changed, I come out to an empty apartment. I waste no time hanging around here. Justin really is twisted up by Meadow, but the thing is she's not his, she's mine, always has been. Nothing can change that.

"Hey." Meadow beams as she opens her door.

"You look good." I return her smile, looking down at her sundress which is fitted nicely around her tits and flows to a stop above her knee. Lucky fucking dress.

"Thanks," she murmurs. I guide her to the elevator with my hand on her lower back.

"So, where to?" she asks, her gorgeous eyes roaming my face. Shit, I'm becoming such a pussy because the butterfly chick crap is happening to me right now.

"I thought we could go to Jay Jay's."

Her cheerfulness falters. Jay Jay's is where I bought her first guitar, we used to go there all the time to check out the instruments. "I don't play anymore, Rift."

I try to read the emotions that have taken over her face. "Why?"

She drops her eyes to her feet. "I just stopped. It hurt too much to play."

My stomach turns over. I really messed her up when I left, and to be the reason she stopped playing and writing is a fucking crime.

If I wasn't me, I'd string me up by the balls.

I reach forward, stroking the tip of my finger down her cheek, grasping her under her chin and tilting her head to look at me. "I'm so sorry I left, Beats. I was in a bad place and it just kept getting darker. Please, let me take you to Jay's. I want to buy you a new guitar. I want you to play again. Let the hurt go."

Her eyes gloss over and a tear drops to her cheek. It breaks my fucking heart to be the reason for her tears. She sniffs and then giggles at herself for being unladylike. "You're right, I need to let go."

My stomach rolls at her words. Does she mean let go of the past or let go altogether?

Once we get to Jay's, her face lights up. She lets her finger glide over all the guitars hanging on the back wall. I reach up and pull down a black acoustic fender and take a stool from a set up drum kit.

"She has unique colored eyes that can tell no lies,
She has the perfect nose,
Lips the color of a red rose,
And I love her from her top to her toes."

She bursts into laughter. "I can't believe you remember that."

I lower the guitar and smile back at her. "Hey, I wrote that in under a minute when you asked me if I loved you."

She's smiling back at me, a hundred memories in her eyes. "You did."

I hand her the guitar. "Your turn. Do you remember your reply?"

She bites her lip and shoos me from the stool then takes a seat. "Fine, but I'm beyond rusty nowadays." She strums her hand down the strings.

"I love when we touch,

It can never be too much.
The way your fingers brush my skin,
You make me tingle from within.
The feel from your lips, the stroke of your tongue,
I'll love you forever, you are my one."

I'm completely solidified. Hearing her sing our stupid little song that she made up on the spot the day we told each other we were in love is keeping me still. Her eyes bore into mine as she strums the last note and I just want to grab her up and run away with her. How could I have left her?

"Well, fuck me sideways." I turn to see Jay striding through the shop. He reaches his hand out and I gladly shake it. "Where have you been, man?"

I shrug my shoulders and turn back to Beats. She seems lost in thought.

Jay leans over me. "Shit, you're both here. Come here, girl." He pushes me aside and takes Beats by the hand, pulling her to her feet and kissing her cheek as he wraps her in hug. "You haven't been here for way too long. We missed you."

A smile touches her lips. "I'm sorry. I haven't played in a while."

"Well, that's a crying shame because you kids had talent, you know? Drake's band has been picked up by a record label."

"For real?" I ask, impressed. Drake always had talent.

"Yeah, he's leaving for New York next week. You should stop by and see him, he would love to see you guys. In fact, he's coming into the shop later today."

"Well, we're going for food but I want to buy Beats a guitar so we'll pop back in a bit."

We go to a small bistro a couple of shops down from Jay's. I place our order, ignoring the obvious flirting of the young waitress as she invades my personal space while placing my cutlery in front of me. Beats notices too and sniggers at me.

"What's funny?" I ask with a smirk.

"Oh, nothing. I just find it funny that the waitress rubbed up and down you while giving you your fork."

"She has no shame. I'm here with another female and yet she still makes a play."

"Maybe I should come and pee around you. Mark my territory," she says, raising an eyebrow.

"You don't need to go to those extremes. I know who I belong to."

She stiffens and then fidgets with her napkin. "So, your Mom and Drew huh?" I ask, to take the awkwardness away.

"Yeah. It's crazy. I never thought she would settle down and I never realized her and Drew ever had a thing. I kind of guessed when he took her in after she got evicted, and your Dad mentioned" Her head shakes like she's clearing a memory a false smile sets in place "but marriage? I never saw it coming."

"So, what happened with Justin, when I left?"

Her eyes flick up to mine and she shifts in her seat. "Your Father told him he caught us together. Didn't Justin talk to you about all this?"

"He only asked if something went down with us. I told him no and then I didn't hear from him until a month ago when he asked me if I was coming here for the wedding."

"He told me you weren't coming. That you've settled down with a girl and have no reason to want to come back here."

"He played us. If you knew I was coming, would it have made a difference to the outcome that night?"

She sighs. "I got wasted because of what Justin said, so yeah I guess, maybe. God, this is a mess. I don't even remember going back with Justin. How stupid was I? I guess I was lucky he took care of me. I can't make excuses. I was reckless and could have ended up in a gutter somewhere. I've learned my lesson."

I fight back the retort and venom wanting to strike out about him. I'm pissed at him. She was wrecked, but if she was so out of it, what the fuck was happening in Justin's mind to still take her to his bed. How desperate to be with her was he?

"Rift, you're grinding your teeth," Beats tells me as the waitress places our plate of French toast in front of us.

"Enjoy, and if you need anything just let me know," the waitress says, rubbing my shoulder.

Beats watches her leave. "Wow! I think you could probably do her over our table right now the way she was flirting."

Hearing her say that has visions flooding my mind of me bending *her* over this table. Hmm, flipping that little sundress up, grabbing onto her fine ass and ramming into her sweet tight pu...

"Rift!"

I shift in my seat and sit forward to hide my growing erection. "What?"

Her eyes are wide. "You groaned."

"Maybe you shouldn't talk about me fucking someone over the table. You're putting thoughts in my head."

Her mouth drops open. "Wow, if you want to get her number or something, I'm sure she would oblige your fantasy, pervert."

I grin big. "She wasn't the one bent over the table in my fantasy."

I relish in her innocence as the blush creeps over her cheeks. God, she's beautiful. I missed her.

"Eat your food, Rift," she tells me, her voice higher than it usually is. She's still affected by me and that puts a huge smile on my face.

"Bloody hell. I thought Jay was screwing with me when he said you two came in here," Drake says as we walk through the door of Jay's. He charges Beats and pulls her into a bear hug. "Damn, you're still ridiculously hot woman." She smiles at him. "When are you going to dump the Jacobs boys and give someone else a chance?"

I punch his shoulder. "Hey, I hear you're going to be a rock star.

You'll have a million girls, and then you can stop chasing mine."

He grins and looks back at Beats. "Yeah, but she's one in a million."

"You're not wrong. So we're here to get her a new guitar."

"Yeah, Jay told me. I'm glad you're going to play again. I'd love to get together when I'm back in town and maybe talk about doing some writing together," he tells Beats.

Her eyes nearly fall from her head. "Wow, I haven't written in a while but I'd love that. I don't live here anymore though, so I'll have to give you my phone number so you can let me know when you're back."

His smile makes me want to kill him, hit her over the head, sling her over my shoulder and disappear with her to my man cave.

"Sounds good."

I pick up the black Fender for her and tap her hands away from my card the whole time I pay for it. She accepts it with a promise she will never stop playing again.

By the time we get back to the hotel it's past seven. "Movie and room service?" Beats asks, placing her new guitar on the bed.

"Sounds good. I think we have the last Die Hard film we need to watch."

"Okay, good. I'm going to shower and change. You order food." I trial her with my eyes as she goes into the bathroom before I pick the phone up and place our order of two burgers and fries.

When she comes out of the bathroom, her fruity scent from her shower wash invades my nose. God, she's wearing little shorts and a tiny t shirt. "Are you trying to give me blue balls?"

Her face turns crimson and she looks down at herself. "Am I showing too much skin?"

I swallow. "No, you could never show too much. You're beautiful."

She tucks her hair behind her ear. "Thank you, but maybe this wasn't a good idea, I'm pretty tired. Do you think we could maybe take a rain check on the film?"

I want to kick my own ass for being so bold and frightening her into pulling back from me.

"I'm sorry. Can't we just rewind this conversation and pretend it didn't happen?" I ask, optimistic.

"I'm tired, Rift. I had a wonderful time today and I love my guitar. Thank you."

I take the hint that she needs space. I climb from the bed and cup her face, bringing my lips to her forehead. "Night Beats."

MEADOW

I MANAGED TO avoid both Jacobs's boys yesterday after spending the day with Jared the day before. All my feelings for him have become heightened. I need space, to reign in my emotions. I can't spiral down that rabbit hole again; I'll never find my way back. So I stayed away, despite his many attempts to see me. Today is the wedding and I'll be forced to see them both.

I check out of the hotel and make my way over to Drew's. The place is all decorated in ribbons and balloons for the reception.

"Nice of you to show up," Mom says as I dump my suitcase behind the bar.

"Is there anything you need help with?" I ask, ignoring her bitter tone.

"No, everything's ready now. Help would have been nice yesterday. Just get your dress on, the cars will be here in an hour."

She's walking around in her underwear, her hair pinned up with a few loose curls tracing her neckline. Her subtle make-up makes her look younger than her years.

"You look good, Mom."

She stops pacing and looks over at me. "This is it for me, Meadow. I love him and I've changed into a better person because of him."

We stand in silence for a few minutes before I turn to go get ready.

She picked my dress for the color; it's violet like my eyes. Satin, sleeveless, tight and finishes a few inches above my knee. There's a black ribbon fitted under my breasts, and despite the shortness, the dress looks good. I pin my hair up to match hers and apply some mascara and lip gloss. I slip on my black stilettoes and make my way downstairs.

"Oh, you look gorgeous," Mom says, taking me in. I try not to gape at her giving me a compliment and store it away in my very few, good things she's said about me folder. She's wearing an A-line white wedding dress.

"So do you."

"The cars are here," Ellie informs us, and we make our way outside. It's just me and Mom in the first car. I have no idea who the other cars are for.

We arrive at the town hall and I'm approached by Justin; he's wearing a suit and looks handsome. His hair is neatly styled but I can't help looking past him to Jared. I catch my breath when I see his wearing a suit, his hair a dishevelled mess giving him a rougher, sexy edge. God, he is so gorgeous.

"Meadow, we need to talk. You've been avoiding me. I've been going out of my fucking mind."

I tear my eyes from Jared and look at Justin. "There's nothing to talk about. You lied to me."

He reaches for my hand. "I know, but I need to explain my reasons."

Jared, Max and Maria all spot the scene Justin is creating and they quickly walk over to us.

"Justin, what's going on? Who is she to you? I thought she was a one night stand of Max's but I'm not stupid. You've been acting weird since that day."

She grabs onto Justin's arm and his head drops. "Meadow, are you going to talk to me?"

My eyes flick past him again to Jared. Justin notices my focus fall on his brother and he sighs. "I can never compete with him in can I, Meds?"

I reach up and hug him. I'm done arguing. He lied but God, this is the story of our lives. We love, lie and leave each other and we all hurt from it. I don't know when I will ever see him again and I go with what my body wants and that's to offer him a little comfort and in return gain some. The blonde's hand falls from his arm. He embraces me and squeezes.

"I really missed you and it was good seeing you again but I'm going back home as soon as the wedding's over, the same way I came. Single."

That's my way of letting him know there isn't a choice to make. He has a girlfriend and Jared has his own life to get back to. I break away from him and see the blonde has stormed off. Jared has also vanished.

I go inside the building; there's an impressive white marble staircase leading up to the wedding venue. A few of the wedding party are standing around, waiting. "Have you seen my Mom?" I ask Ellie.

"I think she's downstairs. There's a room allocated for the bride to wait in, I'll show you."

I follow her down, and she points to the door then goes back up the stairs. I go over to the room and open the door. The walls are painted cream. There's a vanity table and a chair, a small window letting in the soft glow of the sun, and black railings in front of the window to prevent break-ins, reminding me of the window in Drew's office at the bar.

"So, are you going to take him back after everything?"

I spin around to see Jared standing behind me.

"You didn't lock the door," he says.

He strides towards me, forcing me back against the railings of the window, his breath hitting my face as he speaks. "I heard him talking to our Dad, at the hotel, saying he's going to leave that Stepford wife girl because he loves you, and then you were hugging him outside. Is he who you want, Beats? Does he make you feel the way I do? Does he make your heartbeat skitter, your body come alive by just being near him?" He places his fingers over my erratic pulse in my neck. "Does he make you heat up? Does he dampen those panties?" His other hand moves to my inner thigh. His finger brushes over my pussy and I hold my breath. You wanted it to be me in that bed, Beats. You wanted to feel my tongue on your body." He brings his mouth to my neck and licks the sensitive spot below my ear.

"Oh, God," I moan as he tilts my head back. He lifts my arms above my head.

"Hold on to the bars," he growls into my ear.

"No," I breathe back, but I comply and hold the bars anyway. He moves his lips down my neck, across my chest to the top of my breasts. He yanks my dress down slightly, exposing them. My breathing accelerates as my chest heaves towards his waiting mouth. He captures my nipple between his lips with a growl reverberating from his chest.

"No, stop. I can't," I weakly protest, while lifting my leg up his hip.

Jared's eyes pierce mine with a lustful stare. We're so close, my breasts on display for his devouring. His groin pushes between my legs.

"I can't do this, the wedding starts soon," I tell him, trying to get him to back off but he just grins and tugs my dress up to my hips. My breath catches and sparks ignite my skin, sending a pulse of heat through my body. I can't help but lick my lips. Lifting my hips to his waist, my legs curl around him.

"Don't move your fucking hands, Beats. Hold on." Unbuttoning his trousers he releases his hard cock then rips away my panties with a quick tear. He lines himself up at my entrance and plunges straight into my wet heat. I let out a scream of pleasure; I'm so ready for him the entry doesn't hurt. It's tight and feels amazing.

Feeling him inside me floods my body with so many emotions it's hard to breathe. He pulls back then thrusts back in. It's hard to keep hold of the railings with the sheer power of his thrusts.

"Oh, God," I moan as he continues to thrust in and out of me, his cock teasing the sensitive spot on my front inner wall with every stroke. His mouth captures a nipple, sucking hard, grazing his teeth over my tight bud. His fingers dig into my ass for leverage. "Rift, that feels so good," I pant.

He steps backwards, taking my hips with him, arching me as his hands hold my lower back. "Don't let go, Beats," he commands as he steps back again.

I'm stretched out; my body suspended in the air as my hands grip the railings. He thrusts in and out, hard and fast before slipping free, leaving me empty and needing more. He raises my hips and buries his face between my thighs, making me erupt in continuous moans of pleasure. My legs grip over his shoulders as he laps, kisses and sucks at my clit. He dips his tongue inside me, groaning when my scent coats his tongue. My body is shaking; my pussy convulses.

My arms begin to burn, growing tired. "Oh God, I can't hold on," I plead.

He thrusts his tongue harder, building the explosion in my core. Just when I'm tipping over the edge and think I can't hold on any longer, he lowers me down and spins me around. "Grip back on, Beats."

I do as I'm told. I now face the bars and he thrusts back into me from behind. My body tightens around him as an orgasm rocks my body. I scream out as he plunges deeper, reaching around with one hand to trace circles over my clit. My body explodes into the most intense orgasm of my life, my legs going weak, quivering all over.

"I'm coming," I cry out.

He shouts my name as his hot release pumps into my body.

I slump forward, holding on to the bars to keep myself upright.

I feel his lips on my back, his hands roaming all over me.

"Meadow, are you in here? The service is starting," I hear Ellie call though the door.

"Okay," I croak, trying to right the sex mess Jared has me in. I straighten my dress and look down at my torn panties. "Rift, I have no panties now and this dress is tiny."

He grins and scoops up my ruined panties, stuffing them into his pocket. "You'll have to sit with your legs crossed."

I rush past him to the small bathroom at the back of the room. Once I'm cleaned up and looking presentable I unlock the door and slip out.

When I reach the wedding party, they're already seated. Ellie looks me up and down. "You look flushed. You feeling okay?"

I smile and take my seat. "Fine, thank you."

The service is over quickly and before I know it, we're back at the bar. I manage to slip on a fresh pair of panties from my suitcase while everyone is welcoming the new bride and groom.

I don't know what the pre-wedding sex means for me and Jared but all I know is his eyes haven't left me; they're devouring me. If a look could make someone combust, I'd be ablaze right now.

My desire sizzles when I see his Dad arrive. My skin crawls, infested with his toxic presence. I didn't think I would be seeing him here, Drew said he wasn't invited. Seeing him still has a terrifying effect on me. His eyes catch mine and he looks at me with cold intent. I avert my eyes as quickly as possible and help out behind the bar; it's getting busy with guests.

The night passes quickly. I end up staying behind the bar most of the night. With it being a free bar, it's constantly packed with guests wanting drinks and it keeps me busy and away from the prying eyes of the one Jacob I can't stand. I hadn't seen him at all apart from the once when he arrived. I hoped Drew had seen him and asked him to leave.

I watch Mom dance and laugh with Drew all night. It's nice to see her so happy. Maybe she really has changed and things will be different.

The night winds down; people have left and only the main family and stragglers occupy the bar. I notice Mom's not around but Drew is. I open a beer for Max, slide it along the bar with a wink and head out back. "Ellie, have you seen my Mom?"

"Yeah, she went outside for some air."

I open the back door and hear voices arguing. I follow the sound and find Mom arguing with Jared's Dad. "Oh, look. Here comes the mini whore."

I freeze, fear forcing me to stop. "Go back inside, Meadow."

"No, stay where you are." My body shakes as he approaches me. "Did your Momma tell you she was fucking me a few weeks before my stupid ass brother proposed to her? She thinks she can be more than the slut she is." He laughs and it chills me to the bone. "She can't be a wife. I'll have her bent over my car by next week, and if you think I'm going to let my son ruin his life on a skank like you, you can think again."

Venom pours from him as he reaches up, grabbing me around the throat. Memories of the last time he attacked me surface, making me panic and struggle to get free. I dig my nails into his hand. "Bitch," he hisses. One hand releases me but then a crack stings my cheek, making me gasp. Pain explodes as he leaves a fire blazing in the shape of his hand on my face.

"He wanted to dump his nice girl for a tart like you. You are sin, Meadow. Made to test me."

Mom pulls on his arm. "Let her go you asshole."

He shrugs her off and smirks. "Okay." He lets go with a shove.

My stomach somersaults as I fall backwards and realize there's nothing under my feet. I reach out, grasping air and tumble down the concrete stairs, scraping my skin against its harsh surface and landing in a heap on the floor.

My head falls back with skull-crunching force, making contact with a thud and robbing me of sight, sound and consciousness.

"YOU CAN'T ALL be in here."

"Well, we aren't leaving." I hear Jared's voice but he sounds distant, like he's in a tunnel.

My eyes flick open. My vision is blurry and it takes a few minutes for the room to come into focus. I see figures standing around me before I realize I'm lying in a hospital bed.

"She's awake." Justin comes into view. "Hey, how you feeling?"

I flex my body and everything hurts. "Sore."

"Beats, what the fuck happened? The police arrested our Dad. Did he hurt you?" Jared asks.

"Her Mom already said he didn't, Jared. Stop trying to force lies on her just to spite Dad."

"Fuck off, Justin! You're so blind when it comes to him."

"You're just bitter and want to take the only person I have left from me, and I won't let you." He turns his eyes to me. "Med, don't listen to him poison you. You can't send Dad to prison for him bumping into you by accident when he was drunk. Don't take him from me, Meds. I've lost enough." I see the fear in Justin's eyes and it breaks my heart. He is so frightened of being alone he can't see what a monster his Father really is. I understand his fear, I have been alone my whole life, my mother was a there in form but God, she didn't have maternal instincts and she was never interested in learning how to be a parent. It leaves a hole that no one can fill when you don't feel love from the people that created you. Justin had his Father love but he didn't know the sickness that lived in him, and just like my Mom didn't want to learn about being a parent, Justin, didn't want to see the truth behind the anxiety I had always had towards his Dad.

"What did Mom say?" I ask, curious as to why she hasn't already told them what happened. My voice breaks as I speak. He could have killed me! Right in front of her, for a second time and she didn't protect me. I should learn by now about disappointment, but it hurts every time someone who's supposed to care about me, lets me down.

"It was an accident," I hear her say as she steps up to the bottom of my bed. I didn't even realize she's here. She's pleading with me with her eyes. "He will tell Drew," she whispers. The final thread of my childhood self, clinging on to the hope she would one day want me, love me tethers.

Both brothers look at her. "What does that mean?" Jared asks. She shakes her head. "Did he hurt her on purpose?" he bellows.

"Stop saying that, Jared! He wouldn't hurt a woman. You're trying to manipulate the situation to get revenge on him for having an affair. He wouldn't hurt Mom or Meadow."

Hot tears slide down my face, causing a fire trial in their wake. "Mom, is this really what you want?" I need her to confirm it one last time, and she nods. Indifference for her washes through me, cleansing me of the sting of her betrayal. "Fine, I won't press charges."

Justin exhales hard. "He wouldn't hurt anyone on purpose, Meadow. You're doing the right thing."

I pull myself into a sitting position, wincing from the sudden pain shooting through my head, and look at my Mom. "You've never been a mother to me." She drops her eyes; she can't even look at me. "You never protected me from anyone. All you care about is yourself."

I turn my eyes to Justin. "I know I hurt you, and how much you love your Dad, and that's the only reason I won't press charges but this is it between us. If we do ever see each other, don't mention him to me again. He is a vile man who strangled me until I passed out when I was sixteen, when he saw Jared leaving my house after finding out he was a cheat."

I hear the sharp intake of breath from Jared. The atmosphere chills and thickens. "He called me names and intimidated me whenever he could. When Jared left the second time, he tried to force himself on me. That's why I was topless and my clothes were ripped in your bathroom that day." I swipe at the angry tears staining my cheeks. "Did you never wonder about that, Justin? Or did you just ignore it like you always did when he talked about me behind my back?" Justin has unshed tears forming in his eyes; he's shaking his head in denial. "Tonight he grabbed me by the throat and pushed me down the stairs in front of my Mom, and she's more worried about Drew finding out she still puts it about than protecting me."

Justin pushes away from my bed and flees the room.

"I'm going to kill him. I'm going to fucking KILL HIM!" Jared roars. "I can't believe you never told me any of this, Beats!" He's pacing the length of my bed. "You can't let him get away with it. It's an insult to you, me and everything he put my Mom through."

"I can't do that to Justin," I murmur.

"Beats!" he bellows, smashing his hand down on the side table. "When are you going to stop doing everything to suit Justin's feelings? What about how I feel? Do you even care?"

My tears continue to stream down my cheeks. "I've hurt him enough. I can't do that to him, I won't."

Jared brings his face close to mine. "You're choosing him again, Beats. Do you realize that?" He storms away from the bed. "I'm not staying around for you to break my heart again. If you let him off from this I'll fucking kill him with my bare hands." He looks to my Mom. "And you're a disgrace." I watch his back as he walks away from me again.

"Just go, Mom," I tell her as she tries to approach the bed. She doesn't hesitate as she scurries from the room. I take in a few deep breaths to try and calm myself. I will never get used to being left by him. How easily people can walk away from me leaves a shadow on my soul, haunting me, taunting me. I was never good enough to make Rift stay, my Mom love me or Justin believe me.

A plump nurse enters the room, smiling at me. "Hello there. I'm glad your guests have left, I was just going to get security."

She checks some buttons on a machine next to me. "You took a nasty fall but no broken bones, just a few bruises and a bump on the head. We want to keep you overnight to keep an eye on you." She wraps a strap around my arm and begins to pump it up until its squeezing the skin and making my arm feel numb.

"Do I *have* to stay the night?"

She writes something down on her clipboard. "Your blood pressure is fine. You don't have to stay, but we do recommend you stay twenty-four hours when suffering a head injury." I pull back the covers and notice a small tear in my satin dress. "We can get you a gown to change into."

I shake my head. "I'm not staying." I scoot my ass to the side of the mattress and attempt to stand. I feel a little woozy but it passes. I thank the nurse and head to reception to discharge myself.

I stumble from the reception area and out the exit door; the fresh night breeze hits my face. I inhale it into my lungs, promising myself this was the last time that man will ever touch me. If he ever tries again I will kill him myself.

I jump into a taxi after it drops someone off. I give the driver the address for Drew's bar and close my eyes as he drives me there.

I'm almost asleep when he says, "We're here, sweetheart."

My eyes flutter open, and pulling the handle on the car door I scoot out. "I just need to go and get some money."

He opens his door and comes around to me. "You okay, sweetheart? Let me help you." He grips my elbow and helps me into the bar. The doors are open and I'm grateful I don't have to knock. The bar is empty except for Drew who's sitting at the bar with a bottle of whisky. He turns when the door opens. He rushes over to me, taking me from the cab driver. "What are you doing here? I thought they were keeping you overnight."

"I couldn't stay there. Have you seen Jared?" He looks down at me with sympathy on his face.

"He left, babe."

My heart plummets. I knew when he walked away at the hospital I had lost him again, but it still hurts to hear it spoken out loud. I turn to the cab driver. "Would you mind taking me to the airport?"

"Of course not, sweetheart."

"Drew, can you bring my suitcase out? It's behind the bar."

He strokes down my arms. "You sure you don't want to stay? You're pretty banged up."

I shake my head and hurry back out of the bar. I slip into the cab and wait for Drew to bring out my suitcase. He hands the cab driver some money and kisses the top of my head before shutting the door and tapping the roof to signal for the driver to leave.

MEADOW

"MY BROTHER WANTS you, Med. You know that."

I smile as we leave the hotel to walk to the bar where Crystal's brother is playing with his band. I know he likes me and tonight I'm going to give him some attention.

It's been too long since I had some fun; over two years since I got totally drunk and ended up being foolish. So I had a spa treatment to make myself feel more attractive, and put on my best outfit.

Crystal and I enjoy numerous shots while we get ready. I'm feeling buzzed and ready to let my hair down for once.

JARED

"OH, CHECK THEM out. Fuck me."

I look over at the two women standing at the bar but only one holds my attention. Long chocolate colored waves flowing down to her waist; her legs are toned and long, peeking from a short black dress that's sculpted around a perfect perky ass like a second skin. Her hips sway gently to the riffs coming from the band playing on stage. The beats pick up into a steady tempo, her hips sway, grinding to the music. Damn, she can move. Every eye in the bar is on her. I feel the familiarity pulling from my soul to hers. Her friend is cute too, but not like *her*; she glows with sensuality. Her hand goes up as she feels the beat of the music. She lets out a shout of approval and gains shit-eating grins from every band member on the stage. My heart is thumping against my chest and I have no idea why. This can't be Beats and chicks don't have that effect on me since her. That shit passed years ago.

"Shit, she's smoking hot. You think she's a bar bunny?" Jinx asks, gaining looks from everyone at our table.

"You ever seen a bar bunny that looks like that?" I ask. I've haven't been drinking so why was I hallucinating.

"Man, I wish we did,"

The music slows and finishes. She claps her hands. "Woo, you rock!"

"I think she's wasted," Silver states.

"Hey, baby! Why you don't bring that fine ass over here?" Rex calls out to her.

I hold back the retort that they could only get a girl like that was if she was wasted. It's just about to leave my lips when she turns her head to us. My stomach turns to mush. Her eyes lock onto mine. The noise fades out, the lights seemed to have dimmed and there's nothing but me and her locked in intense disbelief and, as always, pure desire gaze.

"Shit, you seen the way she's looking at Rift?"

"Shut the fuck up," I snap, and stand to go to her. My strides eat up the distance. I grab her hips and jolt her towards me. Her breath hitches, her hands splay across my chest.

"What the hell are you doing in a bar like this, Beats?"

Her eyes bore into mine. She looks around "I came to support my friend's brother. He's in the band."

I look over to her friend who is swaying from too much drink, and yet she's still tipping back shot after shot. "He your man?"

She shakes her head no then realizes I have hold of her. She forces me to let go. "What are you doing here?" she asks, clearly affected by me still.

"This is where I play." She looks to the stage then behind me at the table where my band and some boys from the club are sitting. "What the fuck are you wearing?"

She looks down at herself. "A dress."

I cock an eyebrow. "Barely, babe."

Her eyes squint at me. "Screw you, Rift. I don't need this."

She tries to walk away but I grab her by the wrist. "I haven't seen you for years and that's all you've got to say to me?"

Her friend leans over her shoulder. "Are they your friends?" she slurs, holding her glass in the direction of my table.

"Yeah, sugar, but I suggest you stay away from them."

"Whatever, handsome." She giggles and wanders over to where my boys are.

"You missed me, Beats?"

Her eyes flash. "You ass, I haven't seen you because you once again left me" she hisses.

I can't help but smile sadly at her. "My brother told me you disappeared after the wedding. Why didn't you come with me, Beats? I just needed to cool off, I was fucking pissed"

"Because you didn't ask me to. And the way I remember it, you took off, not me."

Her eyes gloss over. There is pain there and my heart hammers against my chest as she speaks. "Did you miss me, Rift?" Her voice is barely a whisper.

"Every fucking day." I roam my eyes over her perfect face, stopping on her lips. She's clearly intoxicated making her body speak for her and not her mind. She wants to punch me and kiss me all at once and I know how she feels because I want to shake her and fuck her all at once. Why the fuck did we do this to ourselves, the fire between us was undeniable. Our souls belonged together, I was only ever fully satisfied when I was in her presence.

"God, how can you be here? Screw it, let me go or kiss me, Rift."

My eyes shoot to hers. Shit, she really said that. I waste no time. I pull her into me and crush my lips to hers. She's as sweet as I remember; more so. Her tongue dances with mine. Her teeth bite down on my lip, pulling a hungry growl from me. Cat calls from my boys ring out. I can't pull her any further into me but I need her closer. I need to consume her. Ravish, explore, and savor her all at once. "Let's get out of here, baby," I moan into her mouth.

She turns to the bar, slams a shot down and drags me out the door. "Where's your car?"

"I drive a bike, baby. Over here." I pull her to the back of the bar where the private parking for our bikes is.

"A Harley?"

"What else?"

Her chest is rising and falling with heat and excitement from our make out in the bar, and I can't help myself. I pull her to me and ravish her mouth.

Her hands fist in my shirt, my hands grab at her ass. I lift her to straddle my waist and she doesn't think twice. Her dress rises up around her hips as her legs wrap around me. I hold onto her with one hand and throw my leg over my bike so I'm sat straddling it and she's straddling my lap. I lean her back and let my eyes take in the sight of her panting, lying on my bike. Her lacy panties are in full view for my greedy eyes. I brush over them with my hand.

"Fuck me, Beats. You're so wet for me already." I slip my thumb under the material. Her silky smooth pussy contracts at my contact. "You're bare."

"Yeah, Rift. I like it bare."

"Me too, Beats."

I scoot my ass back and lean forward, tearing at her panties. She jerks and gasps at my aggressiveness, then her hands go to my hair and she tugs, showing me what she wants. I smile up at her before bringing my mouth to her smooth, wet pussy. Her hips tilt up to meet me with every thrust of my tongue. I lick every inch of her, paying special attention to her throbbing clit and when I feel her clench, I thrust in two fingers. Her hot, slick walls welcome me, squeezing me for more. Her pussy clutches onto me, pulling me into her further. Her moans are loud, like music to my ears.

One of her hands leaves my hair and grips the handle bar, her hips grinding up against my face. "Yeah, fuck my face, Beats. Come in my mouth, baby."

"Argh, yes, yes!" she cries. I feel her shudder and come all over my fingers. I slowly draw them out, lapping at her leaking juices.

Once she settles down from the high of her orgasm, I reach under her back and pull her up. Her body moulds against mine, liquefied. Her hair falls around her face like a curtain of silk. She's looking at me with heat in her eyes. Her tongue darts out and swipes across my damp lips. She bites her bottom lip then whispers, "I taste good. How do you taste?"

I nearly blow my load right there. "Get on the back of my bike, Beats."

I lift her and shimmy her ass around until she's behind me, her thighs clutching me tightly. When I walked her out the bar she didn't sway or falter so I'm confident she's not too wasted. She will be safe to ride and she'll remember every inch of her body I devour tonight.

I roar the engine, ignoring the vibrations against my aching balls, and take off. Her hands stroke up my body, her nimble fingers seeking skin on skin. I can't get to the compound quick enough. The gates open as I approach. I park and pull her from my bike. I push through the door, the music rebounding off the walls, a buzz of rowdy, horny people humming in the atmosphere.

"A bar?" Beats murmurs behind me.

I nod my hellos to everyone.

"You want more company, Rift?" Candy purrs, and gropes my chest as I push past. She sees Beats and her hands drop.

Yeah, take a good fucking look because no bar bunny has shit on Meadow, she's grade fucking A. I gain approving nods from my boys.

I don't slow my mission to get Beats naked. I reach the stairs and pull her up them. I reach my room and push the door open then kick it closed behind us.

"What is this place?"

"It's my home, baby," I tell her, reaching for the hem of her dress. I slip it up her body and step back to take in her naked form. Her skin glows; she has a natural tan to her body, she's toned and smooth. Her tits are natural and full, something I don't see often. Her flat stomach has a silver guitar charm dangling from her belly button. "You're pierced?"

She looks up at me. "Well, it's not a clip on, Rift."

I continue my appraisal of the sexiest woman known to man.

Her sculpted legs and dainty feet complete the full length of her 5'6 frame. Her heels are still on and it's fantasy worthy. "You are so beautiful, Beats."

Her breathing has become heavy. "Take your clothes off, Rift. I've waited too long for this."

My eyes go to hers and I stride to her and pick her up. I throw her on the bed and her hair fans out across the mattress. I reach for my top and pull it from my body. I undo my belt and watch as her gluttonous eyes take in the sight of me. She bites her bottom lip and I want to explode right on the spot.

She sits up and starts undoing my buttons, she tugs them open and shoves my jeans down, freeing my cock. "Commando?" She smiles.

I don't get a chance to answer because her hot mouth closes around my cock, making me lose my breath and my mind. I grab at the nape of her neck with one hand and grasp her hair with the other. She takes me into her mouth deep, fast then slow. Her tongue slides up the base to tip then dips into the slit.

I groan and tug her away. "I need to be inside you now," I growl. I grab at her hips and lift her further onto the bed. My mouth smothers hers, my hands groping her tits, pinching her nipples between thumb and finger. Her body shivers as mine ignites.

"Please, Rift."

I bring my lips to her nipples. "Please what?"

"Please," she moans as I bring my thumb down to her throbbing clit. "Rift, I need you, please," she begs.

"What do you need? Tell me and I'll give it to you." I feel her body tense and shake as an orgasm rocks through her body.

"I need you inside me now!"

I dip a finger inside her wet folds and her hips grind against my hand. "Is this what you want?"

She's panting hard. "God, Jared. I want your cock," she growls.

I remove my finger and thrust straight inside her, making us both call out. She feels unbelievable, her tight pussy squeezing my cock, her hips grinding and thrusting, meeting everything I have to give her.

I reach for her, pulling her body flush with mine, turning us so she's straddling me, her body rocking hard as she rides me. I slide in deeper than I've ever been and I have to hold her hips still for a few seconds to stop myself from coming too soon.

Her lips attack mine; she nips and sucks at me, then moves down my neck. I loosen my hold on her hips so she can grind them, lifting then forcing herself back down hard with a tilt of her pelvis; up, down, faster and faster. She's incredible. The sweat from her efforts makes her skin glisten. Her hair tickles my thighs when her head drops back, her tits thrusting forward. I reach up to them, pinching the tantalizing buds hard as they call out for my attention. She cries out as her pussy contracts against me. She doesn't stop her fast rhythm, squeezing and commanding my release. Her hands go up into her hair as she whimpers, her body convulsing, her walls tightening and strangling my cock. Her hot pussy releases all over my shaft, making me blow with a roar. Her hips slow, drawing out my conclusion.

I stroke over her sweat slicked skin. She leans forward and collapses against my chest. I hold her against me, letting our bodies recover.

MEADOW

I'M LYING ON Jared's naked chest. My night has not turned out how I expected. I was planning on letting Crystal's brother have some tongue action tonight. He's had a crush on me for a while but instead, here I am. No matter how much time passes I still can't get enough of Jared.

His strong hands stroke my back. I feel his arousal grow against my stomach. "Already?" I ask, impressed.

His heart-stopping smile beams up at me. He rotates his hips and then twists, pinning me against the mattress with his strong body.

His hands entwine with my mine. He holds them beside my head and softly brings his lips to meet mine. Fire ignites in his eyes but like every other time before, I also see his need for me emotionally.

I lift my head to meet his lips and enjoy the soft caress he offers. His erection prods at my entry. I wrap my legs around his waist, giving him permission and he takes it, slowly sliding inside me. He's firm but slow, taking all of me. His eyes bore into mine as his lips taste every part of my face. Lifting my hips to meet his thrusts, our bodies stroking together. His eyes never leave mine as he increases his tempo; his hands remain tight in mine. His breath steams against my skin, his sweat blending with mine, our moans forming a duet of pleasure.

He thrusts hard and I feel myself build and contract against him, pulling at his cock, milking him for everything he has to give. He follows me over the edge with a growl of my name.

Jared collapses on top of me careful not to crush me with his weight. I stroke at the tattoo over his heart.

"Yes," he mutters, his breathing still heavy.

"Yes?"

"Yeah, it's a tribute to you." I scroll over the text.

'The words in my lyrics, the music in my sound, the beat in my heart.'

"It's beautiful," I murmur.

He kisses my nose. "You're beautiful, Beats." He rolls to his side and pulls me into him, cradling me. My eyes get heavy and the room goes dark.

There's a buzzing. It takes me a while before I realize the buzzing noise is a phone. I untuck myself from Rift as he stirs. "That's yours," I mutter, still half asleep.

He groans and rolls to the side table. "What's up? When? No. No, Silver, wait for me. Ten minutes, okay?"

I stroke down his muscled back. "Everything okay?"

He slips from the bed and smiles down at me while reaching and pulling on his jeans. "Yeah, baby. I need to go out. Stay there and sleep, okay?" I pull the covers up to conceal my naked form, and nod. He bends down and kisses me, the passion still in full force. "I need to go. I'll wake you when I get back."

The sun bleeds through a crack in the blinds.

I hear muffled voices getting louder and louder until the door bursts open. A blonde-haired woman rushes into the room, her top showing off her stomach, her jeans tight. She's heavier set than me, her boobs clearly fake.

"What the hell is this then, Razor?" She looks to a tall guy filling the doorway. His dark hair is pulled back into a low ponytail. He has a goatee and striking green eyes. He's wearing leather trousers, a white t-shirt and … a leather cut. I saw Rift put one on before he left, and all his friends at the bar were wearing them too. I thought it was a band thing, but when he dragged me through the club downstairs I noticed they all had them on. I had seen them on a TV character Crystal has posters of, she told me it's a biker thing they call them cuts, she rambled on about some president called Jax and how she wanted to ride him reversed cow girl, at that point I stopped listening. Razor has full-sleeved tattoos on both arms.

"For fuck's sake, Tessa! You can't do this shit here. Rift will kill you!"

"Fuck him! It's been a week since I lost his kid and he's already filling his bed with bar whores."

I wrap the sheet tight around me as the guy in the door stares at me with a knowing grin. "Hey, sweet ass. You want to hop into my bed for a while before you leave?"

I feel like I'm still dreaming; did he really just say that to me? Have I gone back in time to when this shit happened to Justin and me? No this is of a much bigger magnitude. Did that woman say she lost Rift's baby? Did that guy just proposition me, while I'm naked from spending the night with someone else? Will Rift ever stop crippling me with his disappearing act? Where the hell has he brought and left me? Oh God I'm having a meltdown, this is what it feels like to lose your mind. After everything that has happened to me I've finally cracked.

"Hey, why you still here?" I shake my head in disbelief at Tessa. She scoops my dress up and throws it at me. "Get dressed and get the fuck out."

Another guy leans his head through the doorway. He looks at this, Tessa and then at me. "Fucking hell, where did she come from. She new?"

"The bar last night, man. But if she's staying, I call dibs on her ass next."

I just threw up in my mouth. I'm vibrating in my own skin with the need to get away from here.

"Would you all mind going away so I can get dressed?" I whisper.

"Where's the fun in that?" Razor grins.

Tessa huffs. "Get out, let the tramp get dressed." She ushers the men out and follows them.

I rip my dress over my head and pull it down. I jump from the bed and go to the dresser. In the drawers I find a pair of Jared's workout shorts. He must live here. What the hell. Has he changed that much? Is this where he ran too all those times. I pull them on, rolling them at the waist to tighten them so they don't fall down. I pull my dress over them and slip my heels on. Degraded, dejected and the old favorite, pain occupy my mind and heart. Can I believe what the screeching banshee blonde woman said, why would she lie? God he could have had a child with someone else. The cold creeps over my heart trying to protect me but it can't, it never could when it came to Rift. I'd be damned if I was going to keep listening to these assholes treat me like some whore, paid by the hour.

I go to the door and yank the handle. Tessa is waiting for me and so are the other two men, and a couple of new ones have joined the crowd. "Oh, yep, that's the honey he came in with last night. Hey sugar," a blonde-haired guy says as I push past them and down the stairs. I'm one step away from taking my shoes off and attacking the leering pervs with them.

They all follow me down. "The door's that way, bitch," Tessa tells me, pointing.

I turn to her, anger rising like the tide to the surface. She is grating my last nerve. I shouldn't have to put up with this shit, I deserve more than this from him and maybe she's hurting too, but fuck her and fuck him too "Watch your mouth when you're talking to me, and tell Jared I'm the one running this time."

She screws her face up at me. "His name's Rift, bitch."

That's the last straw. I pull my arm back and smack her right on the nose. There's a pop, and blood sprays from her face, coating my dress. It hurts like hell, my knuckles explode in pain but I relish the throb, she earned that.

"I know what his name is. I fucking gave it to him… bitch."

She crumbles to the floor. Gasps and howls pour from the guys in the bar. "Shit, Tessa, she fucked you up," Razor bellows, then grabs my wrist. "Wait. What do you mean you gave him his name? What's your name?"

"Meadow. What's it to you?" I yank my hand from his grip.

"Meadow as in Beats?" he asks. I look to him and notice the whole bar has gone quiet, including the moaning from Tessa. I ignore him and push through the door. I'm shocked to see I'm in a huge building like a plane hangar. I march across what's used as a parking lot and head towards the huge metal gates. There are two guys manning them. "I want out!" I shout.

"Sure, sugar. Make sure you come back though." They grin at me and I feel dirty. I've never had so many filthy eyes undress me before. I walk down a drive and follow the road until I find a cab to take me back to the hotel.

"MEADOW!" CRYSTAL BARKS pulling me from my memories. She's staring at me, her eyes wide. "What the hell? You've been sitting there like a zombie. Are you going to tell me how you know him?"

I get to my feet and swipe at a tear. "It doesn't matter, I won't see him again anyway. He likes to disappear."

She follows me across the room. "Well, if he's sending requests on Facebook, he clearly wants to see you again."

I turn to her. She has been my best friend for two years. We share everything but I've never shared my past with her and she's always known not to ask. "That's his brother not him. They're twins."

She gasps. "Twins? Holy shit, which one is it Meadow?"

More tears fall. She comes over to me, offering me comfort in her embrace. I cry into her hair which smells of smoke and vomit. "I don't know."

"Meds, this is bad."

I pull away and swipe the remaining tears. "It's not bad. We're going home today. I can't go back to your brother's. I need to get back home today so I can forget all about this fucking trip."

I see understanding in her eyes as she tells me okay.

We pack up our stuff and load up her car; we drive in silence until we hear a familiar voice bleed through the radio.

"If I stand in the rain, will it wash away the stains you left on my skin?
Can it wash away the sadness, the pain from within?
Can the rain cleanse me, make me new, and make me good enough to be loved by you?
Can it wash away my memory, wash it clear?
Stop you from hurting me even when you're not here.

Can the wind carry my sins away?
Make you want me, make you stay
Can the wind take away the ache, blow life back into me?
Carry the pain away, set me free?

Can the sun ignite my soul?
Heat life back into me, make me whole
Can it warm my blood, bring a beat to my heart?
Can it warm my body, force it to restart?
Can it burn your birthmark from my soul?
Turn me back to the person I used to know."

I hear a sniffle coming from Crystal. I look over to see tears falling from her eyes. "It's beautiful. God, he really did it. That's your song he's singing."

I smile at her, my heart warming at the sound of Drake crooning my lyrics on the radio.

"Mom we're home," Crystal calls out as we walk into her house.

"We're in here girls."

We follow her voice to find her in the living room. She's on the floor, sitting with Jasmine and Jules who are giggling at her. "Mom, Mom, Mom," they coo as we approach.

"Hey, babies. Mommy missed you both."

I sigh, wrapping them both in my arms, their beautiful amber eyes roaming my face.

"You're home a day early."

"Yeah, Meds missed the girls. Wow, Mom. Who are the flowers for?" I look to see Crystal picking out a card from a huge bouquet. "They're for you, Meadow. Figures." She hands me the card.

Meadow,
You're taking us all the way to the top, beautiful.
We need to discuss more. I'll be home all week.
Can you make it home?
Love Drake

"God, my brother has been blowing up my phone all day. I'd better call him and let him know we won't be at the show tonight."

I reach for her arm. "Drake wants me to go home to discuss the song."

A smile tugs at her lips. "Can I come?"

Jules pulls on my top. I give her my attention, kissing her soft cheek. "What if Justin's there?"

"Meds, you need to tell me everything because I can't be a good friend and give you advice with no details."

I bury my head into Jasmine's neck, gaining a giggle from her. "Okay, you're right. Let's make coffee and talk."

"So, she tried to throw you out and you punched her?"

I nod. "I'm not proud of it, but I've had bitches like her talking to me like crap my whole life and I was so angry."

She beams. "I wish I was there. God, I know it's a fucked up situation but you and this Jared seem like soul mates."

I stare at her, dumbfounded. "From everything I just told you about him leaving, then coming in and out of my life when he pleased, then taking me to that place where his girlfriend woke me up by screaming at me while his friends propositioned me. And me trying and failing to find him when I found out I was pregnant... you think we're soul mates?"

She shrugs her shoulders. "I'm a romantic and a realist. He's super-hot and it seems to me his brother is an ass, always trying to intervene, stopping you two being together."

I rub my hands down my face. "I can't believe I let him take me to that place. God, I was going to have a good time, maybe make out with your brother, and Jared was there. It's like life's playing a joke on me."

"Ew, I don't need to hear anything about you making out with Micky. But I will warn you, he has been phoning and texting me all day, going crazy that you left with some biker dude."

I let out a small whine.

"Meds, your phone is ringing in here, sweetheart," Crystal's Mom calls.

I kiss Jules on the temple and slide her into Crystal's lap to go retrieve my phone.

"Hello."

"Hey, Beats. Did you get the flowers?"

A smile touches my lips at the familiar voice.

"Hey Drake. Yes, I did, thank you. They're beautiful."

"I want you to come home for a few days, we need to discuss

business."

I look to Crystal's Mom who is playing with Jasmine. "I can't just up and leave, Drake. I have the girls to think of."

"Bring them with you. I have a nice bonus check here for you, plus I want to talk to you about you writing some new material for our tour."

"A tour?"

"Yeah. This song is going all the way to number one. Our manager is talking about a huge tour."

"Oh my God, Drake!"

He laughs. "Say you'll come. Please. You and the girls can stay here."

"Okay."

"Okay?"

"Yeah, this is huge. I'm so happy for you and the band."

"When will you get here?"

"Tomorrow. I'll be there tomorrow."

I can hear the smile in his tone. "Can't wait."

I end the call and approach my curious best friend who has Jules planted on her hip. "Drake wants me to come into town. The song is doing well and he wants to talk about me writing some more for them."

She jumps up and down with Jules, giggling. "That's awesome! Can I come?"

"He wants me to take the girls. What if I bump into Mom, or worse - Justin?" I ask, staring into Jules' beautiful face.

"You said he left there."

"He did. When I went to tell him I was pregnant he wasn't there. He didn't go back to Florida either. I don't know, maybe he came back."

She lowers Jules to the floor, her feet hitting the ground and taking off, walking to Jasmine on her unsteady legs.

"You need to decide if you're ever going to tell them, Meds. Why don't you accept his friend request and look up his info on his profile to see where he's living?" My eyes grow wide as I gape at her. "That's such a good idea. I've had that request for over two months." Going to her backpack and pulling out her laptop, Crystal places it on the dining table and flicks it open. The browser is still open from when I slammed it shut earlier. It prompts me to re-sign in. Once I do, I bring up the request and hit accept. "There's nothing on there."

She states the obvious over my shoulder. There's nothing, just his picture. No details, and no other friends.

"Wow, I can't believe I didn't notice it straight away, Meds. The girls look like him." She pats my shoulder. "Or the brother."

I give her a *duh* look. "Of course they look like the brother, they're twins!"

"That's a weird profile. Maybe he set it up just to request you?"

Butterflies stir in my stomach and not in a good way. I close the browser. "Let's go pack the girls a bag."

DRAKE'S MOM IS sitting on her wraparound porch as we pull up, her bright smile beams at me. She calls out to Drake as she approaches the car, then swings the back door open and coos at Jasmine while unbuckling her seatbelt and lifting her into her arms. "Who's my beautiful girl?" she says.

I unbuckle my seatbelt and open the car door as Drake comes outside, his smile solely for me. He jogs down the front steps and takes the couple of strides to where I'm standing, wrapping me in his strong arms and inhaling my hair as he holds me tight to his body. "Hey, beautiful."

Returning his gesture, my arms wrap around his waist. "Hey, handsome."

"I see you brought your roommate."

I crane my neck to see Crystal standing next to the bonnet, Jules in her arms and a huge smile on her face. "Yeah, she kind of has a thing for the band."

His body shakes with a chuckle. "Well, they are coming over tomorrow for Mom's barbeque, so she can get her fill."

A small giggle escapes me. Drake's arm rests on my shoulder as he guides me into the house. "So, Mom's going to watch the girls while I take you on a celebration dinner."

"Oh, can Crystal join us?"

His smile falters but he tries to camouflage it. "Yeah, sure. I'll have to call and change the reservation."

"No, don't." Crystal smiles. "You two go, I'll stay and help with the girls."

Drake's grin grows. "Okay."

I give her a warning glare. Drake has made it abundantly clear that he would like more from me than friendship. He loves both my girls, but I haven't been ready for a relationship. I need to concentrate on earning money to raise my daughters and give them a good life, better than the one I had.

I WALK DOWN the stairs dressed in a knee-length black fitted dress, my hair pulled into a messy up-do, and some curled strands hanging loose around my face. Reaching the bottom step, my four-inch heels click against the hardwood floor bringing everyone's attention to me.

"Wow, you look stunning," Drake says, holding his hand out for me to clasp. He's wearing black slacks and a steel-colored shirt.

"You look good, too," I reply, taking his offered hand.

I let him pull me to the front door and we wave over our shoulders to Crystal who has just settled the girls down for the night.

Drake guides me to his BMW convertible, opening the door for me. Lowering myself in and buckling the seat belt I inhale the smell of new leather.

"You like? It's a perk."

I look at him, surprised. "The car is a perk from your manager?"

He laughs. "They were gifts for our success."

"They? As in you all got one?"

His smile grows into a huge beam. "Yep, and I have a bonus check for you too." My mouth is gaping. I quickly close it and try to avoid his eyes as he keeps stealing glances at me.

He weaves us through the traffic effortlessly. "From one song?" I manage to ask once my shock fades and the silence eats at my nerves.

"We only needed one song to catapult us, Beats. We had some interest from our other few singles but this one has climbed the charts so fast. Now we have people interested in interviewing us, and marketing our products. We have a tour from this, Beats. We're going to be number one. Do you realize how huge that is?"

I let it all sink in and nod. "Huge," I whisper.

He chuckles, reaching a hand over to squeeze my thigh.

We pull up outside the restaurant. My door opens and I step out, thanking the valet boy. Drake hands over the keys and guides me inside with his hand on my lower back.

He gives his name to the hostess and receives a warm smile. She guides us to a table in the back next to a window overlooking a balcony. The atmosphere is relaxed; the diners are all dressed in suits and elegant dresses. This is the fanciest restaurant I have ever been in and it makes me a little nervous. I would have been happy grabbing a pizza and eating it at home with the girls.

The air is thick with the aromas emanating from the kitchen, making me realize how hungry I actually am.

Drake orders a bottle of champagne and two specials, not even looking at the menu.

I sip from the water in front of me, hoping to give myself a few seconds to calm my nerves. I feel a little uncomfortable here. It's a romantic setting; everyone around us is in pairs on dates.

"So, we want you."

I raise an eyebrow, nearly choking on the water. "We?"

"I mean the band and the label would like you to come on board writing with us for our tour and next album."

I'm flattered, and my heart beats faster at the prospect. I work as a receptionist at a small label. It's on the ladder, but nowhere near where I want to be. However, it's a regular income and at least it's in the music industry, even if it's only answering the phones to musicians or their agents.

"I know you need to be with the girls, and you have a job which won't interfere with you working with us. We can carve our time around you."

He's so thoughtful of my situation. He knows how important my girls are and he never pressures me.

"I would love to write more with you, Drake. You know that's my passion and where I want to be in the future."

He stands, cupping my face and kissing my forehead. "The future's here, Beats. The song you wrote is a hit."

He takes his seat, his eyes still on me.

My eyes dampen. "That's huge," I sniffle, still coming to terms with how well the song is doing. His answering smirk and head nod makes me giggle a little at my emotional moment.

The waitress appears with a bottle of champagne, opening it with a pop, startling me and making me giggle more. She pours some into our glasses, leaving the bottle and disappearing.

"To our success." Drake beams, raising his glass, possibilities gleaming in his eyes.

Clinking my glass with his I say, "To us."

Excusing himself, he leaves the table, returning a few minutes later holding a stack of papers. "I left this in the car. It's your check, and this is a contract to say you agreed to write with us."

I take the papers from him, a little surprised he has them on hand.

"I had this drawn up since we put your song on the album. I really want you to write more for us." He hands me a pen.

"Do I need to have my lawyer look this over?" I tease, squinting my eyes at him.

He fakes offence, dropping his jaw and placing a hand to his heart. "It's for you, to make sure you get all your royalties. You can trust me," he assures with a wink.

I jot my name on the line he points to and hand the contract back to him.

The food arrives. I relax and actually enjoy the rest of the evening. The main course was delicious; a steak so tender it fell to pieces on my tongue. Dessert was even better, actually gaining a moan of delight when it exploded on my taste buds. Red velvet cake, my new best friend.

We talk about the Jules and Jasmine, and how I had found us a new house. I explain that Crystal is going to live with us instead of keeping the apartment we share. I want a house with a garden for when the twins get bigger. I managed to secure a mortgage and Crystal is going to look after the girls while I work.

Drake tells me about all the celebrities he's met, and how different they are in real life. We laugh and reminisce about our school years. It's nice, easy, with no complications, which is what I need.

Pulling up outside Drake's Mom's house and turning off the engine, he stops me from opening my door by reaching for my hand. I turn to find he has leaned into my space. My heartbeat picks up speed and before I can object, his lips press to mine. His kiss is nice, his hands cupping my cheek, his tongue probing at my lips for entry. I open them and meet his tongue stroke for stroke; he groans into my mouth and I smile against his lips.

Pulling away he breathes heavily. "I've wanted to do that for so long," he whispers.

"Okay," is all I can say in reply. He chuckles, leaning back into his own seat to gauge my reaction. I'm confused, unsure if I'll ever be ready to be with another man.

"You have amazing lips. That kiss was better than I imagined it would be. You know I've always wanted you, Beats. I always stepped back for various reasons, but I don't want to do that anymore. I want to kiss you and spoil you and be with you. I want us to be together."

I feel myself hyperventilating. I knew he had a crush, but I didn't expect him to lay it out there like that. I don't know what to do with the information. I kind of knew it was coming but didn't prepare myself to have a reply for him.

He studies my face for answers, a crease etching his forehead. Reaching for my face he tries to soothe me. "It's okay, don't panic. It's not a marriage proposal, Beats."

I get myself under control before speaking. "I know. It's just not what I expected you to say. I have two toddlers, Drake." He starts to interrupt but I put my finger to his lips and carry on. "I know you know that already but I can't offer you much of me right now. I have to be a parent first and you are going to be so busy being a famous rock star, and that will come first for you. Neither of us can commit to anything right now."

I lower my finger from his lips, hoping my answer sates him. He grasps my hand. "I know all of that and I'm not asking for commitment. I just want to date you when we both have time. I want to spend that time with you."

I fake a smile. "Okay, I can do that." His face lights up into a grin before he leans forward and takes my lips again.

Crystal, the girls and I stayed for two more nights, but over the few weeks that followed, Drake and I went on a few dates. He flew out to see me or I drove down to see him. It was nice, but with him becoming more famous, we started getting attention from fans and paparazzi when we went anywhere, and that made me uncomfortable. Drake seemed to enjoy putting on a show, touching me and kissing me in public. My face appeared on entertainment websites, which Crystal thought was awesome. Me? Not so much.

I've been avoiding Drake's calls for the last two days, texting him to say work is keeping me busy. In reality, I just don't feel that spark with him, and when I'm not working or with the girls, I spend my time playing the guitar Rift bought me. Unlike last time he left, when I couldn't face playing, when I got back from Mom's wedding all I did was play. I love that guitar. Everything I ever felt for Rift always flows when I play it, helping me to write my best work. It's like a blanket coating me in memories, in comfort, in love.

NO FUCKING WAY. I storm over to Kitty sitting with her skinny ass on Ice's lap, flipping through a girly magazine. I snatch it from her and roam my eyes over the front page.

"Front man Drake Martin from the band Fury, who has been sitting at number one in the charts for the last three weeks, has been pictured on numerous dates over the past few weeks with an unknown beauty.

Drake was quoted as saying he is single only last month in an interview for an online entertainment website, but since then he has remained tight-lipped about his current status. On the identity of the woman he's been pictured with, he has only revealed, "She's an old friend who has always been special to me."

So, get out the tissues ladies, if the cosy pictures are anything to go by, it seems Drake's heart is taken.

Fury crashed into the charts shooting straight to number one with their single, 'Change Me'.

I've read enough. I throw the magazine into Kitty's lap. She and

Ice look at the front page I was reading.

"What the hell, Rift? Why are you interested in girl gossip crap?"

"I know the dude on the front," I reply curtly.

Kitty's screech makes me flinch with annoyance. She jumps from Ice's lap and begins bouncing in front of me like a moron. "You know Drake from Fury?"

I glare around her at Ice who slaps her ass. "Bitch, sit your ass down. You're in a biker bar, not a high school."

She actually pouts. "Fury rock. And I *am* in high school."

My eyes dart around her again to see Ice's face pale. "What the fuck, Kitty? How old are you?"

Please say eighteen, please say eighteen, I chant in my mind.

"Eighteen last month," she says, sitting back on his lap.

Thank fuck!

Shaking my head, I throw a warning glare at Ice for the close call. Ice is twenty-three but still, we don't need this kind of heat. Eighteen is cutting it pretty close considering he's fucked her in every hole she has for the past two weeks.

"Shit, bitch. You said you were twenty one." He pushes her off his lap, making her squeal.

She gets to her feet and puts a hand to her hip. "That was my sister, Misty. She's twenty one."

"Whatever. It's time for you to roll out," Ice tells her.

"What?"

I feel his demeanour shift in the air around us, leaving it chilled and thick. He's rapidly losing his temper and once Ice does that, it isn't fun. He's finished with Kitty, and once he has finished with a chick, he turns cold, hence his nickname. Ice is a cold motherfucker, and for someone so young he has already paved himself a one way ticket to hell and doesn't give a shit when that time comes. He's scary but loyal, and someone I trust with my life.

"I said we're done. Get out."

Her mouth drops open as she glares at him. She sticks her tits out, twirling a lock of her hair around her finger. "You going to call me?"

Un-fucking-believable! This chick is dense.

"Yeah, sure I am."

She accepts his lie with a clap of her hands and waves her fingers at me as she leaves.

"Her age was too close. You fucking check their I.D if you have to, just don't play that close to the fire."

Rubbing his hands down his face and letting out a string of cusses, his eyes lock onto mine. "Agreed."

The drama with Kitty makes me temporarily forget the fact that Drake is plastered on the front of a magazine with his arm wrapped around my woman. A trip home is needed.

I didn't stop thinking about Beats since the day I came home after the night she was here. After receiving a call from one of my boys who got himself into trouble, we ended up spending the night in the cells. I stewed over the fact Beats was at home in my bed and I was locked in a fucking cell. Once I got out, I made it home to find a bleeding Tessa and no Beats. My friends told me Tessa burst in on her, waking her up, calling her a whore and sending her packing. Tessa is a pain in my ass, faking pregnancies and miscarriages, trying to hook herself an old man, but no one wants that bar bunny on the back of their bike so why she thought she could trap me was a joke. I always wrap it, never failed, and with a bitch like her, I wrapped it twice. The only person I have and would ever go bare in is my girl.

I searched every hotel to try and find her but got nowhere and haven't been able to locate her since. Until now.

THE GROWL FROM my Harley fills the air as I pull up outside Jay's. It looks the same as it always has; a red banner in the window saying Sale Now On, and a green flashing neon sign stating the shop is open.

Memories crash into me as I push the door open. The bell rings above my head to alert him of a customer. Jay's eyes come straight to me and a smile tilts the right side of his face. "Look what the cat dragged in," he shouts down the store at me.

"Actually it was the gossip magazines that dragged me here," I retort and watch his eyes take on understanding.

"He waited a long time for a shot at her, Rift."

My fists flex. "She belongs to me, Jay. He knows that."

"Fuck!" he mutters under his breath but I hear it.

"I want his number or address."

"You can have his number." He pulls out a pad and pen and scribbles down some digits before handing it over to me. Pulling out my cell I key in the numbers and hit the green icon. It rings three times before he picks up.

"Yo."

"Is that how you answer a phone?"

"Yeah, when I don't recognize the number and I have crazy ass fans blowing up my phone."

"How do they get the number?"

"How did you?"

"I'm not a crazy ass fan."

"That hurts, man." The smile in his voice is evident as he speaks.

"So, you've been spending time with someone that belongs to me."

His sigh sounds like I just got sucked into a wind tunnel. "She doesn't belong to anyone, Rift. She's a person not an object."

"She's my fucking person, Drake. You knew she was off limits."

"This is bullshit. We aren't in school anymore, and you can't keep her off the market so you can come and go as you please, picking her up and putting her down."

"Now who's making her sound like an object? You don't have a clue what me and her have so I'll let this slide. Now give me her number and address."

"The fact you don't already have it should tell you something."

"Don't play games with me, Drake. I will get her number from you either way."

"You threatening me, Rift? After all these years of friendship?"

"I have business with her I need to get sorted. I won't tell her how I got her information, but I will get it Drake. As a friend, I'm asking you give me it so I don't have to threaten you."

"I love her, Rift."

I want to kill him. The sheer weight of his declaration makes my heart squeeze in my chest. *What if she loves him too? What if I've lost her forever? Why does fate keep dragging us apart?*

"Yeah, get in line," I growl

"I did and I waited my turn. I'll give you her phone number but not her address, her numbers even more than I'm comfortable with, but if she doesn't want anything to do with you, I won't be waiting anymore. I will make her officially mine."

My stomach threatens to eject the coffee swishing around in there. The anger has no outlet because this asshole is on the other end of the phone, and not the end of my fist. Rage twists my insides. "Number," I demand.

I PULL UP across the street from the address, Samuel, a club contact had got from the number Drake gave me. You can find anything out these days when mobiles where on contracts with phone companies and when you had friends who can do illegal shit. The cute two storey house screams Meadow. It's quaint and charming and stands out amongst the rest. It has a small wrap around porch in yellow, contrasting against the white, giving it a little quirk. Totally Beats.

The shutters on the windows are open, and the lights are on.

I swing my leg over my bike and take a few moments to just look over at the house. Shadows move across the windows so I know she's in there. I inhale some much needed air and walk over.

I come to a halt when Beats pulls up in a black Lexus. She steps from the car and my breath catches in my throat; damn this girl affects me like no other. Her hair is tied neatly into a low ponytail and she's wearing a pencil skirt and fitted blouse. She looks like a sexy school teacher; all she needs is a pair of glasses.

She reaches back into the car, giving me a nice view of her rounded ass. She collects her handbag, swings it onto her shoulder and shuts the door.

I swiftly cross the street before she makes it to her front steps. "Beats."

Her hand rises to her chest as she turns with a jump. "Oh my God, Rift! What are you doing here?"

She looks edgy, her eyes shifting to her house then back to me. Her skin has lost its color.

"You got a man in there?" I ask, my voice hostile.

She looks at the house again, then walks towards me, grabbing my elbow and trying to steer me away from the house. "No, no I haven't," she mutters, trying to move me but I stand firm. No way can her little frame move me. She gulps, a mist clouding over her eyes as the front door opens.

Her drunken friend from the bar steps onto the porch holding a toddler. She begins to speak then her eyes find me. Her eyes bulge, her mouth becoming slack as she mutters, "Fuck."

I know I messed up, but the way they're acting, anyone would think I'm the grim reaper coming to collect their souls.

"Mommy," the child calls, holding her arms out. It takes me a few seconds to realize this child is actually calling out to Beats. My head swims, everything disappears and then whooshes back in, nearly knocking me on my ass. I stagger backwards on my feet, completely stunned. My heart's attacking my chest, trying to break free and land at her feet so she can stand on it. She has a kid! With who?!

The front door creaks open further, putting an end to my internal head fuck until another toddler curls around the drunken friend's leg. She looks exactly like the first. Her podgy cheeks lift when she spots Beats. She takes off running to her, arms out, calling, "Mommy!"

I swear my head is about to explode. Beats turns from me, opening her arms as she walks forward, collecting the child from the top of the steps. "Hey, baby," she says as she strokes down the girl's hair and kisses her temple.

Water fills her eyes as she turns to me. My mind is clawing for some explanation. Maybe she lives with her friend and they are so close that her friend's babies called her Mommy as well?

I tear my eyes from Beats to the child in her arms to see if there is any Beats in her. She's staring at me, her thumb tucked into her mouth, her long eyelashes blinking over her auburn color… eyes …

Stepping forward I scan my eyes between the baby Beats is holding and the one the drunken girl is holding. Holy shit! They look like me and Justin.

I lose my footing, faltering backwards as realization hits me like a boulder in the face. All my emotions are there on display, raw, and fuck me I feel a lump in my throat.

"Beats?" I choke.

She lets out a small sob then turns to her friend. "Crystal, can you please take the girls in and feed them?"

Her friend's head bobs up and down as she scurries forward, taking the child from Beats. "I'm so sorry, Meds. I didn't know he was out here. We saw your car and the girls got excited."

"It's okay, just take them in for me."

Crystal hurries inside the house, taking the babies with her. Beats' eyes find mine and she shakes her head. "I'm sorry. When I found out I tried to track you down but you were a ghost."

Anger pools in the pit of my stomach, tearing up through my

veins. "I wasn't the fucking ghost, Beats, you were. I looked for you everywhere over these last two years! No one knew where you disappeared to, not even your Mom. Are you telling me you had my babies inside you and you looked for me?"

She fights back more tears. "I did look for you…and Justin."

I study her face; she looks sheepish. My world collapses around me. The meaning in her statement hits me full force, knocking the wind out of me.

"Are they mine or his?"

My voice doesn't even sound like mine. Something cold has taken me hostage. She lets the tears fall; she's shaking all over, her small frame trembling. "I don't know. It was when Mom got married."

I want to roar at her. I want to punch the fuck out of my brother for ever going near her, and I want to find out if the woman I've always loved carried and raised my babies, or did the woman I've always loved have babies with my shithead brother, destroying my heart forever?

"Why didn't you say anything when we hooked up a few weeks ago?" I shout, making her flinch.

"I didn't get the chance."

I pace the path, needing to move. "Beats, we talked in the bar, I ate your pussy on my bike. I took you to mine and fucked you twice. You had time."

Anger and embarrassment flushes her cheeks. "Do you have to be so graphic? No, I didn't have time. As you so elegantly put it, we were busy doing other stuff. I would have spoken to you if after you *fucked* me, you hadn't taken off, leaving me to be woken up by some screeching bitch and a bunch of perverts asking me to give them a turn before I left!" she spits at me with venom in her tone.

"They asked you what?"

My temper is at boiling point. My brothers wouldn't treat her like that if they knew who she was. "They were pigs, Rift! Where the hell was I?"

Walking forward so I'm one foot in front of her, I lean into her face. "That place is my home, Beats. Those *pigs* are my brothers, my family."

Her eyebrows furrow. "How can you live there? It's a bar."

"It's a club, and I live there because I don't need my own place. I have no old lady and no kids."

Her eyes close then slowly open again. "Why did you come here, Rift?"

"You took off. I told you not to."

"Your skank girlfriend threw me out and you didn't come back."

"She isn't my girlfriend, she's a bar bunny I gave energy to a couple times."

She glowers at me, jealousy firing in her violet jewels. "Nice. So knocking up anyone these days huh? She was pretty pissed and acted like your girlfriend."

A growl erupts from my chest, bubbling and needing an outlet. I point my finger at her. "She was never pregnant! I didn't knock her up, and don't fucking throw your judgment my way when you don't even know if it was me who knocked *you* up!"

Stepping back like I struck her, she tries to compose herself but I read the pain etched in her beautiful features. "You're right, I don't know. But you knew I had woken up with Justin and you still pursued me. I might have been slutty for letting you, but I have two beautiful girls that came from that messed up week."

Shaking my head, I murmur the thing no one has ever seemed to grasp. "You can't have us both, Beats."

Her laugh is manic. "I have neither, and I may love you both but it's in different ways. There was never a choice for my heart. I just had to let my head rule sometimes."

Her words penetrate all the way down to my soul. I'm her heart just like she has always been mine. "I want to know if they're mine, Beats. Even if they're not, they're still my blood."

Putting a hand through her hair, she takes a few steps back, sitting down on the steps. "Okay, that's fair but I don't want to let you in their life if you're going to come and go from one year to the next. It's not fair to them."

Her words hurt. "If those girls are mine, Beats, they will be living with me. I won't abandon my kids and if I'd known they existed, they would know me by now. Instead I've missed loads of their lives."

Her body quivers as she stands, backing up the stairs, holding out her hands in defence. "You won't take my girls, Rift." I step towards her and she screams at me. "Back the fuck up! Don't tell me you're going to take my girls!"

"I didn't say I was going to take them."

"You said if they're yours they will be living with you."

I nod my head. "Yeah, they will, as will you."

A million reactions play on her face. "What?"

"Beats, I came here to get you. We have wasted too many years apart and now I find out that there might be two girls in there made up of you and me."

She breaks, falling to the floor. I rush the stairs and drop down next to her, dragging her heaving body into my arms. She shudders against my chest as I hold her. "This is such a mess."

"We will fix it," I assure her.

Minutes of silence pass. I worship the Gods for letting me have her back in my arms. Her soft heat encompasses me, making me feel whole again.

My phone vibrates against my leg. Pulling away from me she strokes away her tears. "Answer, its fine," she sniffles.

I pull my phone from my pocket. "Who's this?" I bark, answering the blocked number.

"It's Drake."

"What do you want?"

"You already know the answer to that."

I look at Beats who eyes me with curiosity.

"Never going to happen. Did you know about the girls, Drake?"

Beats gasps.

"Of course I did, I've known about them since she went into premature labor. You weren't around."

My hand fists, cracking down into the decking of her porch. "Don't fucking push me."

"Look, I phoned to inform you that you may get company. I had a phone call from your brother. He wanted the same information you did. Seemed only fair to give him his shot."

"So you gave him her number?" The silence told me what I needed to know, he gave him her address the asshole.

I snap the phone shut.

"Was that *my* Drake?" Beats asks. Her calling him that stings like a bitch.

"Yours?"

She rolls her eyes. "You know what I mean."

"Yeah, he gave me your info and it seems Justin must have seen the same shit I did in the magazines because he's on his way here thanks to *your* Drake."

She shakes her head. "I can't believe he would do that and not tell me, and since when do you read magazines?"

"That doesn't matter. What matters is Justin's antenna of me being near you must be twitching because now he's on his way here."

Her sexy as sin legs starts to pace. "That's good. We can do a paternity test and get this over with."

Grasping her shoulders, I put a stop to her pacing. "Listen, I wouldn't be telling you this if he wasn't on his way here, but Justin has changed a lot in the last two years."

"What do you mean?"

Exhaling harshly I tell her the crap I hoped I wouldn't have to. She's light and beauty, and she loves with all her heart. She cares about people even if it causes her pain. "He didn't take what you said about our Dad very well. He gave up football offers and went on a huge bender, cleaning out Dad's credit cards. He drank a lot then when his money ran out he went back to our Father for more hand outs. Dad went missing, just upped and left, and Justin fell apart. He got himself into gambling, and into some scary situations with people you don't want to know about. He blamed me for Dad's disappearance. He couldn't come to terms with the fact Dad just left him."

"Blamed you how?"

"He thinks I killed him."

"What? Why? Why would he think you would do something like that?"

"Because I would. I wanted to, and to be honest, if he hadn't disappeared I might have."

She gasps, taking a few steps back.

I step closer, her scent invading my nose. "What he did to you is unforgivable to me."

Her head begins to shake from side to side.

"Beats, I'm not the same person that left when I was sixteen. My life hasn't been easy and the life I'm in… I've done some bad shit. I protect the life I have, I protect the family I earned and I protect the woman I love. I always have tried to; it's why I left in the first place." Mom's face invades my memories.

"Love?" she whispers.

I cup her face. "You know I love you. It's always been you for me. You're the beat in me."

A lone tear falls to her cheek. My lips kiss it away. She inhales and her sad water-filled eyes look into mine, our lips a whisper away from each other. "I know it's never been easy for us but we belong together, Beats. I know you know that."

"You're wrong. It *was* easy but then you left me broken. How can I trust you won't do that again?" Her breath warms my skin as she speaks. Before I can erase her fears, the front door opens and her friend fills the doorframe, her arms crossed against her chest.

"Hey, I just wanted to make sure you're okay," she addresses Beats. "I made food."

Beats turns to her and offers a weak smile. "Thanks, Crystal." Breaking free from me she walks towards the door and turns to me. "You hungry?"

I nod as I walk behind her into the house.

The house has a warm feel. The cream on the walls is a canvas for lots of photos of the twin girls. My heart beats faster as I see their babyhood play out in pictures hung on the hallway wall. Their smiles are beautiful like their Mom's. God, she's a Mom and has raised these children without help from me or Justin.

Baby giggles fill the air as we turn into the living area. The girls are playing on a red rug laid out in front of a black leather sofa. The walls are a warm red, and family pictures cover them. I observe Beats as she lowers herself down to play with the girls and my heart pounds wildly against my chest as they both cling to her and giggle as she tickles them. Fuck, I never wanted to be a Dad. My own put me off wanting to share any of his genes but as I watch the woman I love wrapped around two baby girls who look like me, I pray they are mine.

One of the girls turns to me, her cute little face studying me as I stand there staring back. I drop down to my knees and hold up a hand to her. Beats smiles and shuffles closer to me, bringing the girls with her. "Girls, this is Jared, Mommy's friend. Jared, these are Jasmine and Jules."

Jules reaches out and grasps my finger. "Two J's, huh?" I smirk.

"Time for a bath," Crystal calls from behind me, and both girls jump up and run to her. Well, it's more of a waddle on their wobbly legs.

"Food," Beats says, standing. I follow her into a small kitchen; she reaches into a cupboard and pulls out two plates. She pulls a dish from the oven and scoops some pasta onto the plates. I take them from her and walk over to the table to place them down.

She goes to the fridge and bring over two beers and two forks.

"So, how do we go about getting tests done?" I ask as I dig into the food.

"We can buy a home kit and send it off to get the results."

"Tell me how you ended up with Drake."

Her fork clatters to her plate. "That's a quick change of subject."

"I want to know how a few weeks ago you were in my bed, and now you're dating Drake. Or maybe you were already dating him?"

"That's bullshit, Jared. I wrote *Change Me* so I've been working with him, and yes, we've been on a few dates."

"Have you fucked him?"

Her gasp makes me regret the non-filter from my brain to my mouth but I can't help it. I need to know how fast she can go from my bed to someone else's. "How dare you ask me that? We've had a few dates and a few kisses, not that it's any of your business. You had some slut bursting in on me spewing all kinds of crap about you! I'm the one who was single. You can screw who you like but I have to be a nun Rift, seriously? "

I grab her hand as she attempts to leave the table. "I'm sorry, Beats. You're right, I shouldn't have asked. It just makes me crazy that I had you then you were gone again and I couldn't find out where you lived. I was going crazy, and you were going on dates with fucking Drake."

"If you're trying to imply that I didn't care, Rift, you're wrong, I felt it too when I saw you in that bar. I thought finally fate would let us be together again but then you left me in the middle of the night, only for me to wake up in a strange place with some blonde screaming at me and jerks you call brothers leering at me. I felt abandoned and cheap, something I never want to feel again. That woman made out like she was your girlfriend and I was hurt. I've only ever been with you and Justin."

My chest tightens. I see the years of hurt in her eyes. Fate has been a cruel bastard to us. But I'm here and she's here and I'll never let it pull us apart again.

"I don't even remember being with Justin in that way." She lets out a dark laugh. "How messed up is that? I never wanted anyone like I wanted you. I loved Justin, but it was never the same way I loved you. Everything fell apart again after that week of my Mom's wedding, but when I found out I was pregnant, I knew I wouldn't ever be alone again. Those girls became my priority. I needed to finish school, get a job and make a home for them. Dating was never something I wanted to do. That night at the bar was my first night out in forever and I'd planned to have some fun. Crystal's brother has a crush on me so I thought I'd make out with someone that wasn't you or Justin for the first time in my life, and of all the places in the world, you were there. I thought it was destiny until the morning after. So yes, when Drake asked me to date him I thought it would be good for me. He's always been good to me, Rift. He knew about the pregnancy and has been in my life since, but he never pressured me for more than friendship. I did some writing for him, and my song went to number one. He was so happy he offered me more writing work and asked me for more than friendship. He wanted to date me and that felt good. Things *are* good, but no matter how good he is, he isn't you."

My whole body buzzes with need for her. "You've never been with anyone else?" I ask, already knowing the answer from her rant. She doesn't remember even being with Justin, so technically she has only ever been with me.

She laughs. "That's what you took from all of that?"

I stand up and pull her towards me, grasping her hips. "I love you and have only ever loved you. Whether those girls are mine or not, I want us to be a family. I'll love them like they're mine because no matter what, they're yours."

Her eyes mist over and I can't bear to see her cry again so I cup her cheek and crush my lips down on hers, tasting her lips, listening to the music of her moans. I lift her skirt up to her hip, guiding my finger over her thighs. She shivers and I love the effect I have on her. I grab her ass, lift her onto the table and slot myself between her thighs, kissing her deeper. She pulls away, breathless. "I love you. Don't leave me again, I can't take it," she pants.

I squeeze her hip with one hand and tilt her head back with the other. "I promise, we're together, Beats. No more running. I love you."

I take her lips again and shift her hips so they're flush with mine. I grind forward so she can feel my hard cock against her heat.

She groans, tilting her hips for more friction. "I want you but Crystal might come down," she pants against my lips.

I smile devilishly at her and bring my hand between her legs. I slide her panties aside and feel her wet pussy waiting for me. She leans her mouth against my chest to muffle her moans as I grasp her panties and with a quick tug, they rip and come away in my hand. I bring them to my nose to inhale her unique sent before discarding them and whispering against her ear, "I'll be quick."

Shock is written on her features as she looks up at me. I unbutton my jeans and pull out my cock. Before she can object, I guide myself between her folds and thrust forward. She gasps and I feel her nails digging into to my shoulders. "Fuck, Rift."

"That's what I plan to do, baby."

I chuckle as I pull back and thrust forward, taking her breath. I lift her ass and pull her into each thrust, our mouths swallowing our moans. I feel her contract against me and I thrust harder, making the table rock and screech across the floor. Her perfect tits press into my chest, nipples hard, making my mouth water to suck them. I reach up and tear her blouse open, dragging down the cups of her bra and devouring the tight pink buds. Her pussy squeezes hard, releasing her orgasm. I plow forward, filling her with everything I have, straining to stop myself from coming. Her feet dig into my ass cheeks as her body moulds around mine.

"Oh God, Rift!"

She reaches the peak of her climax, draining mine from me. I nip her neck, chin and ear as I flood her pussy with my seed.

We're both panting, sweat clinging to our skin, her cheeks a beautiful rose color just like her nipples. "You're so beautiful, Beats."

She smiles up at me then slaps me to move me away. I tuck myself away as she shimmies from the table, smoothing her skirt down and closing her blouse then searching the floor for the buttons that pinged off when I tore it open.

"I need to go take a shower and kiss the girls goodnight. Grab another beer if you want." She grins and hurries past me.

I watch her leave with a smile plastered on my face. She's mine, always has been and always will be. Justin and Drake can bring it on. No one is getting my girl again.

I'M SITTING ON her couch watching an old episode of *American Chopper* when I hear a ringing coming from the handbag Beats left on the door. I slip her phone out and see Drake flashing as the caller ID. I swipe my finger across the screen and bring it to my ear. "Hey, beautiful," he says, and I grimace.

"She's taking a shower, Drake. I got her a little messy."

"You son of a bitch. You're lying. We're dating; she wouldn't jump straight in the sack with you."

I chuckle darkly down the phone. "You're right she wouldn't. It was the dining table."

I listen to him shout out cusses then I hang up the phone feeling pleased with myself.

MEADOW

I LET THE warm water beat down against my face. As much as I know we have tons to discuss, I can't shake the warm glow I feel all over my body. I love Rift and we're finally going to be together.

I turn the shower off and step into a towel, wrapping myself in a cocoon of cotton. I brush my hair and tip toe across the landing to my room. Crystal is sitting on my bed, waiting for me with a raised eyebrow. "He is so much hotter when he's not blurry," she says as I pull out some PJs.

"Blurry?"

She smiles. "Yeah, when I saw him I was wrecked."

I laugh, remembering her nursing a hangover the next day. "He told me he loves me and wants to make a go of things."

Her mouth drops open. "What about the blonde? And Drake?"

I sigh and plant my ass next to her on the bed. "The blonde was a misunderstanding. And Drake's not Rift."

She rubs my back and stands. "Well, you know I'll support you, and I do think you're soul mates, even if Drake's a rock star."

She saunters from the room with a dreamy sigh. I dress and tip-toe to the girls' room. They are both asleep in their cot beds. I stroke them both gently on the head and leave their room to pull out the spare duvet and pillows from the closet on the landing.

As I hit the bottom stair, I hear Rift talking on the phone, telling someone he won't be back for a few days. My heart rate increases and butterflies take flight in my stomach again. I go into the living room and see him leaning back against the couch, one arm resting along the back, one foot resting on his knee. He looks *so* good. His hair is messy from me running my fingers through it. His faded loose jeans sit on his hips and his black t-shirt hugs his perfect body. When his golden eyes find mine love flows from them. His lips twitch up into a smile. "Hey, baby, you smell sweet."

I sniff my hair and shrug. "It's strawberry conditioner."

He holds a hand out to me. I drop the spare blanket and pillows on the end of the couch and take his hand. He pulls me into his lap and nuzzles his lips against my neck, making me shiver. "So, we have lots to talk about," I mutter.

"Mmm, like what?" he asks, still nuzzling.

"Like where you live, and the distance it is from where I live."

"That won't matter."

I pull away from him so I can look at him while we talk. "Why won't it matter?"

"Because I'm going to buy us a house."

"I have a house."

He sighs. "A house where I live, baby. I can't be too far from the club."

My stomach knots. "I can't move, Rift. I have a mortgage and a job here."

"You won't need the mortgage or the job. I'm going to take care of you all."

I shift to gain a little space between us. "I want to work. I can't just drop everything and take off."

He is insane if he thinks that after he has been here less than a day, I'll pack up and move across the country.

"I want you with me, baby. We've wasted too many years apart."

I know he's right. We have wasted too much time apart, but this is too much, too soon. "We need to think. Let's take it one day at a time for now. Let's get the paternity test done first."

His face drops worry creasing his brow. "I told you, the result won't change me wanting to be with you and the girls."

I kiss him then pull away. "I know, but let's just get this out of the way before anything else."

He stares at me for a few seconds then turns his gaze to the blanket and pillows. "What's with the bedding?"

I'm glad for the change in conversation. "It's for you to make a bed up here."

His eyebrow cocks. "I will be in your bed with you."

"I sometimes have to put the girls in with me at night. I don't want to confuse them by having you in my bed."

I brace myself for him to get mad but he smiles, bringing his lips to mine and kissing me gently. "That's fair enough. For now, anyway."

We get snuggled up and watch a few episodes of *American Chopper* then I slip up to my room before his tongue and roaming hands convince me to stay.

I wake as the sun creeps through my window. Climbing from the bed I tiptoe on to the landing to find Rift standing in the doorway of the girls' room. I sneak up behind him and rub my arm over his shoulder. "Hey," I whisper.

He's leaning on the doorframe, arms folded over his chest. "Hey. I just wanted to watch them sleep. I needed to make sure they weren't a dream."

I lay gentle kisses on his back and wrap my arms around his waist, content for the first time in years.

Justin

MY GPS TELLS me I've reached my destination. I look up at the small house and can't seem to get out of the car. It's been two years since I last saw Meadow, when she told me my Father was a monster. He denied what she claimed to be true, and told me she was a whore who came on to him and couldn't handle rejection so she lied. I know seeing her again is going to pull me back into a false sense of security. She always makes me feel like I'm not alone, even though I am. Everyone leaves me in the end. How bad a person must I be to have everyone leave me so easily?

I couldn't believe it when I got a phone call from Drake. I hadn't heard from him for months, then he called me telling me he found Meadow and she has things she needs to tell me. My heart stopped when he said her name. I've tried looking her up over the years but could never find her. God, I don't even know if my heart can take seeing her again. I dropped my hand on the table and left the poker game I was involved in as soon as he gave me her address, then I drove through the night and now I'm here. I am sitting in my car too scared to see the woman who messes my head up every time.

I open the car and smooth down my crinkled suit. I make a move towards the entrance when the front door opens. There she is, her violet eyes watching me move towards her. She looks more stunning than I've ever seen her; her figure is flawless and her hips are more rounded, showcasing her tiny waist. Her toned legs hold a natural tan. She looks confident in her black shorts and cream blouse, her hair pulled up to give me a glimpse of her elegant neck.

"Hey you," she says as I reach her porch. She closes the distance and puts her arms around me. I embrace her and hold her against me, inhaling her familiar scent.

"Hey." She pulls from my hold and asks me to sit with her on the step. "You don't want me inside?" I ask.

"I don't live alone so I want to speak with you privately first."

My heart hammers against my chest but who am I kidding? She's gorgeous, of course she doesn't live alone. It's only fucked up me that can't move past her. "Okay." I sit on the top step and she follows suit. Her hand goes to my knee and I feel like she's about to tell me someone died.

"So, you saw the pictures in the magazine too, huh?" she mutters.

Confusion stumps me. "Magazines?"

"Isn't that why you're here?"

"I'm here because Drake called me. He told me he found you and you have things you need to tell me."

Her mouth pops open and forms an O shape. "Wait, what do you mean found me?"

I rub my hands down my face. "I've tried looking you up over the years. I kept in contact with a few people from home. He was one of them. He knew I looked for you over the years." Her face has lost all color and tears fill her eyes. "Hey, Med. Don't do that."

She shakes her head. "Justin, I've also been in contact with Drake for the last two years. He told me he didn't know where you moved to."

Anger pulses in my veins. "What?"

"He knew where you were all this time?"

"I don't understand why wouldn't he tell me," I say, completely mind fucked by the realization that my friend purposely kept me from her.

"He had feelings for me but I didn't for him. I had... other things." She sighs and clasps her hands together as she looks straight ahead. I'm trying to digest the fact my friend betrayed me when she drops a bomb. "I was looking for you because after that week of the wedding I found out I was pregnant." My stomach twists into a knot. "This is really hard for me to say to you and I know you will think I'm slutty, but Jared and I were together that week too."

I let out the breath I was holding. "What are you saying, Med? You have a kid with my brother?"

She lowers her head. "I don't know which one of you is the Father. And, actually, I have two kids."

My heart sinks. Two? So she has moved on, and has a kid with someone else as well.

"They're twin girls," she clarifies.

"Twins?" I choke out.

"Jasmine and Jules." Shit, I need a drink.

"So, Jared doesn't know?"

Meadow shifts nervously. "Actually, he saw me in a magazine with Drake so he found me."

"Wait, what? He has my number, why hasn't he called me?" I stand because my temper won't allow me to sit still any longer.

"He didn't know. He got here yesterday. I want to do a paternity test, Justin."

My stomach drops. "I can't believe this is happening."

She stands up and puts her hand on my arm. "I'm sorry. I know this is a shock and you have a right to be mad."

The front door opens and Jared steps out, his hand resting on Meadow's shoulder. He pulls her towards him, kissing her forehead and swinging her into him.

"I thought you said he got here yesterday?"

Her face flushes. "He did."

Un-fucking-believable. "So what, did you just pick up from being sixteen again?" I ask with acid in my tone.

She pulls from Jared who tries to stop her. "There has always been something between us."

I stop her. "When you say us, are you referring to you and me 'us', or you and him 'us'?"

Her face drops and Jared steps towards me. "Don't be a prick, Justin. There are two little girls in there. This is more than any of 'us' anymore, but whatever the results of the tests are, Beats and I are going to be together."

Meadow's eyes drop to the floor.

"Listen, I'm going to the pharmacy now to pick up those tests. I looked it up online, there's one nearby that has them." Jared speaks directly to Meadow. She gives him a nod of her head, and he leaves, walking past me without even a look in my direction.

"So, a lot has changed since last time we saw each other," she says.

Looking in the direction that Jared went in, I shake my head, trying to clear it. "Yeah, and a lot hasn't. Some things never will change, huh, Med?"

The front door opens again and a girl steps out. She looks across the street. "There's that car again, Med." I follow her gaze, as does Meadow, to a black Sedan.

"Oh my God," Meadow says, making the hairs on the back of my neck rise.

"Who is it?" I ask, stepping down the front step and striding towards the car. It pulls out with a screech and drives off at an unnecessary speed.

"It kept turning up outside our old apartment, and we assumed it was someone visiting one of our neighbors, but it showed up in other places I went," Meadow says.

"Did you call the police?"

"No, nothing has happened. I just thought it was coincidence."

"It's freaky now, Med," Crystal says. "This is our new house, there's no way that's a coincidence."

My phone buzzes in my pocket and I slide it out and put it to my ear.

"Walk away from the porch," my Father's voice speaks into my ear. I look around, twisting my head from side to side. "We need to talk. There's a diner a mile up the road from where you are. It's called Jessie's Diner. Meet me there in ten minutes. Don't tell them where you're going."

My stomach feels like a washing machine on a spin cycle.

"Sure," is my only reply before sliding the phone back into my pocket.

"Everything okay?" Meadow asks.

Yeah, just peachy. Ghosts are resurrecting and the past is revisiting to smash the shit out of me. The pain in my chest is an old friend and it came back as soon as I saw her eyes again. "Yeah, I just need to sort something. I'll be back to do the test in a little while."

Her smile drops. "You don't want to meet the girls?"

"It's a lot to take in, Meds. I just found out they exist, and that no matter what, Jared will be there Dad, so…"

She lowers her lashes and pushes her hands into her shorts pockets. "That's not true. I would never do that to you. If you're their Father then YOU'RE their Father, regardless of me and Rift."

I offer her a weak smile before turning to leave.

THE AROMAS FROM the diner make my stomach growl. I haven't eaten since I got the phone call from Drake telling me about Meadow. I need to have words with that son of a bitch, but it will have to wait because sitting in a booth on the worn fake-leather bench seat is a man who disappeared nearly two years ago.

I stride towards him and slide into the seat opposite. An overweight waitress comes over, dropping a cup to the table and pouring steaming hot black coffee into it. "You eating?" she asks.

"Pancakes, bacon, and scrambled eggs." I tell her before she walks off.

My Father grins. "I've missed you." I'm struggling to form words when he continues. "I know you're surprised to see me."

"Surprised? I thought Jared had killed you and buried you in the desert."

"Why would you think that? Jared's not man enough to kill me, and he has no reason to want to," he says, confident with himself.

"For the shit with Meadow."

His eyes darken at the mention of her name. "That whore lies and she's been turning him against us for years."

"Don't call her a whore, Dad."

His palm slams down hard on the table. "You're still sticking up for her after everything she took from us? Now she's raising more girls to turn into whores! She isn't what you think she is, Justin, she never was. She used you, and she hurt you over and over. Now she's going to take you for child support and run off with your brother. They've been plotting for weeks."

"He only got here last night, Dad."

His laugh is mocking. He pulls out something from his pocket and throws it at me across the table. Picking it up, my mind absorbs the image of Meadow laid out on a bike and Jared between her thighs. My hand tremors, holding the evidence of their lies.

"This was a few weeks ago." He points down at the picture. "Putting on a show."

I hold the picture up between my finger and thumb. "You're the one who's been following her?"

He shakes his head in disgust. "She is the one taunting me, Justin. She always was! She put on that show for me to see and now she's playing you again by rubbing it in your face that she's picking him over you. They planned it, and now it's time to get payback."

"How?"

My mind sinks further into darkness. I listen to him talk while I wait for my food to arrive.

MEADOW

RIFT'S DELICIOUS, WARM body is pinned against my back as he nibbles my shoulder. We're naked; sweat moistens our skin from our love making.

Justin has left, taking the DNA tests he and Jared took earlier with him. He's dropping them in the post on his way out of town. He said he needs time. I'm okay with that; he's had a lot to take in, and seeing me and Rift together on top of that wasn't fair on him.

"What are you thinking about, baby?"

"Nothing," I lie.

"How did you carry two babies in this body and not have any marks to show for it?" he asks, stroking up my stomach. I trace his hand, laying mine on top of his as I guide him to the small silver line where my bikini line is.

"This is my mark. I went into early labor. I was only six months so I didn't have time to get huge. Crystal swore by this bio oil stuff, and made me bathe in it. Therefore, no stretch marks, just the C-section scar."

"I want to take you to my life, Beats. Show you the good side. The glimpse you got was not it. You're my woman. You'll ride on the back of my bike. My boys won't ever treat you like they did that morning."

I'm nervous. I have a job, a house, I have Crystal, and I know what he is implying. When he says *take me to his life*, he wants me to live there. To give up everything I have to be with him in his world. My heart pleads to be there with him, but my head rules me now. I'm scared to allow my heart to make decisions for me again.

"We're having a barbecue over the weekend. I want to take you and the girls."

My breath hitches. "I don't think the environment is good for the girls, Rift."

"Baby, we're a family. A lot of my brothers have wives and kids; it's not all about the club. Please. Let me show you."

I turn in his arms to face him. His hand wraps around my waist, the other moving into my hair.

"What do you actually do there? For money, I mean," I ask.

"I handle our accounts and I have a hand in the running of a few other businesses. The bar you met me in the other night is ours. I won the deeds in a poker game. I play there with the band, we're quite well known." He smiles. "But anyway, that's club business. Stuff you don't need to know."

I pull away from him. "If you want me and my babies to move and be a part of your life, I do need to know this stuff."

"Baby, it's a different life to what you're used to, and you need to understand that club business stays within the club. We don't do pillow talk about this shit. You will be moving with me, no choice, and you'll gain a whole new family from it. You'll learn as you go that it's a good life and you'll always be looked after. You *and* the girls."

"Okay, I'll come to the barbecue. But if I don't like what I see, I can't promise I'll stay."

I wake to him strumming my guitar, the soft glow from the sun highlighting him like the God he is. He shifts in his seat by my window, roaming his gaze over me. "Do you play this, baby?" he asks.

"Always. I love it and what it represents."

He strums a few more cords. "What is that?"

I pull the covers away from my naked form. His eyes flash with desire as he soaks me in. "That you're the music in me, whether we are together in person or not. You're my soul, my riffs, you're in every lyric, every strum, and every breath I sing."

He places the guitar back on its stand and strides towards me. He spends the rest of the morning inside me.

"HIS ASS LOOKs good on the bike, Med. Damn I want one," Crystal says while looking out of the windshield of my car.

We're following Rift to 'his life'. I made Crystal come because she is my family and we do everything together. I need her.

I grin and give her a quick glance. "The bike or the man?"

She stares forward. "The man on a bike," she clarifies. We both break into a fit of giggles.

The girls' steady breathing hums from the backseat where they are sleeping the journey away.

"Oh God, I'm nervous," I say as Rift rolls to a stop in front of the metal gates I fled from four weeks ago. They clank and open. He continues forward, signalling us to follow. My blood jolts through my veins, making me a jittery mess.

Parking the car, I step out on shaky legs. I can hear voices and music even though I am at least twenty feet from the bar. Rift strides towards me with a grin on his face. He drops his head and captures my lips with his. "You ready, baby?"

I bite my bottom lip and shrug, making him chuckle. Once we've got the girls out of the car, Rift says, "Come on, baby."

Taking my hand he pulls me forward, looking over his shoulder and jerking his head towards the club. "Crystal, you won't get fed standing there, woman. Move your ass."

She quickly steps in line with us. I take a deep breath as Rift drops my hand to open the door to the club. Holding it open with his foot he re-clasps my hand and pulls me inside.

The space is empty except for a couple of older-looking guys sitting at the bar. They tilt their chins as we walk past. We go through a narrow hall and out of another door into a huge garden. There are people everywhere; men all dressed like Rift, women of various shapes and sizes all wearing jeans and tight tees. Kids' laughter fills the air, and light rock music plays in the background. It's like a huge family gathering.

I look over to where a bunch of mean-looking guys are barbecuing on a huge grill. When their eyes fall on us my, stomach clenches.

"Holy shit. I never thought you'd get her back here." A deep voice sounds through the crowd of people who have gathered around us.

"She took some convincing after being propositioned by your ugly ass, Razor" Rift jokes.

Laughter breaks out, cutting through the tension.

"Sorry, sweetheart. We had no idea you were his actual woman. We thought he'd just got real lucky one night."

The guy they call Razor bends forward and drops his lips to my cheek. "Glad he finally found you." He grins and I smile in return. Jules' face burrows into my neck; she's shy from all the attention around us.

"Hey," a blonde woman says, pushing through. "I'm Lou, Digger's ole lady. Let me show you where we have a play area set up for the babies."

I look at Rift who nods for me to follow her.

Throughout the day I was introduced to many people whose names I won't remember, but they were all really great. They had personalities a lot like Rift's, which meant a lot like mine. We laughed and joked all day. Crystal was content under the watchful eye of a gorgeous guy named Ice. Rift never left my side and I learned that while these people seemed like scary-ass perverts when I first met them as an outsider, when you are on the inside, they are very different. They're protective of each other. They laugh, joke, eat and drink together. They're a family, and I'd never had that, neither had Rift so I could see the appeal.

Lou insisted we stay the night at her house because she had the extra room for the girls. She lives in a beautiful five-bedroom house only a mile from the club. I settled into one room with the girls and made Rift take the other as Crystal decided to stay with Ice. I wasn't happy when Rift informed us that Ice isn't a settle-down guy, but she's a grown woman and she informed us that she isn't looking to settle down, she just wanted to get down on him.

By the time we get back home late on Sunday, it is to an angry Drake sitting on my porch steps. He jumps to his feet when he sees us pull up.

I jump from the car and rush to him. "What the hell? No phone call, no texts?" he asks.

Rift's bike pulls up behind my car and Drake's eyes flick to him. "You jump straight back in with him without even a phone call to me. We were starting something, Beats, and I had to hear him talk about fucking you when I called you!"

I look from him to Rift.

"What? When did that happen?"

Drake grabs me by the shoulders forcing me to look at him. "You couldn't phone me to talk about this?"

"Get your fucking hands off her," Rift growls.

"This has nothing to do with you," Drake spits back.

"You're insane if you believe that." He shoves Drake backwards, forcing his hands to drop from my shoulders.

"Stop!" I order as Rift steps towards him again. "Drake, why didn't you tell me you knew where Justin was? You knew I was looking for him."

He looks at me. "He was going down a dark path, Beats. You didn't need that in your life."

"You had no right to decide that for me."

"I've only ever looked out for you."

"Only if it benefitted you. You wanted in her panties, and why the hell would you give Justin her address after hiding it from him all that time?" Rift snaps.

"You had already got her address, I know how when you and your brother are together fighting for her attention you both end up fucking it up for each other! And I won't deny I've always had a thing for her, but I helped her when I wasn't getting anything out of it. She got a shit load of money writing for me."

Rift laughs but there is only intent to harm in the tone. "You got a number one single from her writing for you. Don't think you did her any favors."

Drake turns to me. "We'll talk more when the tour starts and I have you to myself without him polluting your mind."

Rift lunges for him, grabbing him by the collar and getting right in his face. "Watch it, Drake. You're already on my shit list. I don't want to mess your face up in front of my woman. That's the only reason you're still standing right now, but there's only so much restraint I can show."

I reach for Rift's arm. "Let him go." He looks at me, a softness taking over his features as he releases Drake.

"Drake, I told you I can't do the tour. I have the girls."

He points his finger towards me, his chest heaving from being manhandled by Rift. "It's in the contract, Beats. You have to do it."

My stomach drops. "Why would you do that? You said I could trust you. You knew I couldn't go on tour with you."

"Well, we could have worked that out when you were my girl, but you dropped me for him; the guy who passed you to his brother whenever he got itchy feet and left town."

Drake's feet leave the floor as Rift gives him an almighty punch in the face. I yelp as Drake spits out a mouthful of blood. "You son of a bitch. I have a gig tonight."

"You want to write for him, baby?" Rift asks me.

"I think we should part ways," I tell him, and Drake's eyes meet mine.

"Don't look at her, you look at me," Rift says. "Lose the contract, Drake, or lose the ability to use your jaw. You can't tour if the lead singer can't talk, let alone sing."

Drake stumbles up to his feet and pushes past us, retreating to his car.

IT HAD BEEN two weeks since we sent the DNA tests. We paid extra to have them rushed through so we were waiting every day for the postman. Rift had spent those weeks with us, getting to know the girls who were smitten with him as was Crystal. She had told me she'd ever seen me this happy and she was right; life seemed right again.

*

Rift brought back so much that was missing in me. We completed each other, so when the postman came and delivered the news that Justin Fathered the girls and he fled the house, my heart stopped and an old familiar dread crept into my veins.

He was gone for four hours and thirty one minutes before he walked back in to my house and told me it didn't matter. That we were still a family and he would be the best uncle the girls would ever have, want or need.

I shattered into a million fragments as my heart combusted in my chest. He wrapped me in his embrace, bringing all my pieces back together but I still felt a sadness deep in my soul that he isn't their Father.

I rap my knuckles on the wooden front door. Max seems confused when he opens it and sees me and Beats standing there.

"Hey," he mutters, bewildered.

"I take it Justin didn't tell you he's back in contact with me?" Beats asks him.

"Nah, but it makes sense now. He was waffling about you the other night."

My fist clenches. "Well, are you going to stand there and gape at her or let us in?" I ask, pushing open the door and stepping around him. He moves aside, letting Beats follow me.

"Come on in," he says sarcastically.

"Where is he?"

"He's out. He's only been back here a few weeks. How did you even know?"

"We'll wait, and it doesn't matter how I know."

Beats' phone chirps and as she slides the screen, a smile creeps over her face. I raise an eyebrow and lift my chin to communicate my intrigue. She flashes the screen to me to show a picture message from Crystal of the girls curled up asleep together.

"Shit, you two got kids?" Max asks, looking at the picture Beats is holding up to me.

My stomach twists and Beats' face falls.

"Justin really hasn't told you anything, has he?" she asks.

"I can't get much out of him apart from drunken bullshit about you."

A haunted look creeps over her face and my temper begins a slow sizzle.

"Well, you remember my Mom's wedding, the night we went to out to the club?"

Max smiles. "Yeah, I remember the red dress you wore and the next day when I first met the scary version of Jared."

"I will become a lot scarier if you mention what she wears with that smile on your face again." Fucking little shit.

Beats places her hand on my chest. "Yeah, well I left the apartment that morning with three heartbeats."

I want to punch his face in when his brow furrows.

"I don't understand."

"Are you fucking stupid? Justin knocked her up that night."

If it's possible, his face twists with confusion even more.

"But you didn't sleep together, so how can that be possible?"

Feeling comes back into my body when I realize he may not have known that they had actually done the deed.

"DNA results beg to differ, jackass," I growl at him.

"What do you mean we never slept together?" Beats asks. "You shared that apartment with us that night."

"The fact that I shared the suite is how I know, Meadow. I came in just after you two did, and you were arguing about something he said. Shit, let me think… oh yeah, he asked if you would know who it was this time, whatever that meant. You freaked out on him and threw shit. Started stripping your clothes off and crying, saying you were going to bed alone. I sat up with him while he nursed a bottle of whiskey. He had just gone into your room when ten minutes later, *he* showed." He points at me. "Unless ten minutes was enough. But then why was he bitching the other night about how he was meant to be your first and how ironic it is that he still…" His eyes shoot to me and he looks sheepish when he continues. "Hasn't felt what it's like to be inside you."

Beats drops into a chair and I start pacing. None of this makes sense.

"They did a paternity test." Her voice is laced with shock.

Max shifts, scooting back his chair and standing to get himself a beer. He tilts the bottle towards me as he pulls it from the fridge. I shake my head.

"Is that the swab thing he was fucking around with a few weeks ago?" Max asks.

Beats' back straightens and her head swings in my direction. I shake my head and shrug. "What do you mean?" she asks.

Max seems unfazed by all this as he slowly lowers himself back into his chair. "He was messing around with these envelopes that had cotton wool type swap sticks in them. He acted all skittish and secretive when I asked what they were and stuffed them in his bag." He tilts his chin towards Justin's black duffle bag propped up against the couch.

My pulse accelerates in my veins. Things don't add up, and before I can process anything, Beats propels herself across the room and starts pulling things from the bag. She falls back on her ass and pulls our tests out. I stride over to her and grab them from her hands; they're both here, the ones we both completed at Beats' house, her handwriting on the front. Justin's is still sealed but mine is open and the swab is gone.

"I don't understand." Her voice is barely a whisper.

The front door opens and in walks Justin, looking dishevelled. His eyes drop to Beats sitting in front of his bag, his clothes in her lap, and then his eyes rise to meet me and he pales.

I hold the tests up. "What the hell's going on, Justin?"

He throws his keys on a console table and sighs, closing the door with his foot. I follow him in to the kitchen where he pulls a glass from the cupboard and pours himself a drink.

"Start fucking talking, Justin."

His eyes fall on Beats as she comes into view standing next to me. "I don't understand," she murmurs, pain evident in her tone.

"I've always loved you from the first day you stepped from that creaky rust bucket car and your violet eyes smiled at us. Even before your lips did. Damn, you were beautiful and you just got more stunning, Med."

I pace and glare at him. Beats steps closer to him. He knocks back the drink and pours another. "It stung like a bitch when you and Jared finally admitted your feelings for each other, but to see the light in your eyes made it bearable." He looks at me. "Then you fucking left us, turning out that light." He closes his eyes for a few seconds and pounds the full glass back. "You took my brother and my Mom when you left, but you also took a part of Meds, too." I hear a small sob break from Beats. He smiles at her. "You cried so much for him, I had to keep tissues in my bag for when you would break down all of a sudden if someone mentioned him in school, or if a song came on the radio. Then finally, little by little, you stopped crying and began to live again. I waited for you and God, you were worth the wait." He steps towards her, lifting her chin with his finger. "Every touch, Meds. Every kiss was worth how long I waited to have you, to finally feel your love."

I step towards him, forcing him to drop his hand from her and step back. He glares at me. "Then *he* came back and stole your love back."

She shakes her head. "That's not true, I'll always love you," she whispers.

"Just not the right kind of love. Not like you love him," he spits, glaring at me.

"Get to the fucking point, Justin" I say.

"The fucking point is, you took everything from me. My brother and Mom when I was sixteen, and Meadow over and over again. And then finally, you took Dad."

"Dad is a violent asshole, he isn't worth your bitterness. Mom was ill and needed to get away from him. As for your brother and Meadow, we're both standing in front of you."

His face screws up. "You know Dad blames Meadow for us hating each other, and I let him convince me that maybe Meds is evil."

She gasps and I step closer to Justin so we're almost nose to nose. "Evil?" I growl.

He shoves me backwards. "Yeah, Dad's convinced Meadow's Mom raised her to get revenge on him. He said that's why Meds was with us."

He's not making sense. "But he didn't know her Mom before the day we met Beats."

He laughs, tipping the glass to his mouth. "Nope, that's not true. Dad said he knew her when she was pregnant. Apparently she tried to lie and say the baby was his."

Beats steps forward, her expression has gone from sad to angry. "That's bullshit. She was already pregnant when she moved there, so how is that possible?"

"I don't care about the details, Meds. All I know is Dad thinks you've been playing us for revenge. He said you came on to him, flaunting your body around our house whenever you stayed. Playing me and Jared against each other to divide us, making Jared leave and take our Mom to punish Dad for choosing her over your Mom."

"That's insane."

"Then you continue to play us off against each other over the years. He said I'm more like him and he loves me more so you made me suffer more than Jared. Getting pregnant then only wanting DNA when you knew I came into money so you could take me for every penny."

I can't take much more of his insanity. "You're crazy."

"What money?" Beats asks, confused.

He laughs and looks to me. "Jared knew I won big. Dad said you planned the killer blow. You and him planned it together well before I turned up that day. Raise my fucking kids together on my money, except those girls aren't mine, but you didn't know that did you, Med?"

"Justin, this is absurd. You and Jared found out at the same time. He showed up the day before you."

His face contorts. He throws his glass across the room and it shatters into pieces; the brown liquid oozes down the wall. "STOP FUCKING LYING," he roars, making her flinch and step away.

"You better back the hell off!" I warn him.

"He showed me pictures of you two together weeks before, outside a bar."

My stomach shifts and I feel bile rise in my throat. "What?"

He puts his hands on the counter and his head drops between his shoulders. "You and Med on your bike, like she's some cheap whore."

My fist reacts, and before I realize it, Justin's on the floor, blood trickling from the side of his mouth. "You ever call her that again, I'll kill you."

"So, the tests?" Beats asks, her voice weak.

"Dad said we couldn't let you raise the girls into whores and that I should go for custody. When I told him I couldn't be their Dad, he came up with the plan to switch the tests, getting revenge on both of you."

She gasps and drops to her knees. I want to cradle her in my arms and whisk her away from this madness, but then it sinks in that the girls are mine. I feel overwhelmed, my heart swelling for my girls, but my head screaming at me to kill Justin for trying to take them from me.

"Justin," Beats whispers, scooting closer to him. "How could you believe him? How could you do that to me?" Her sobs break through and she brings her hands to her face as her body shakes with sorrow.

"I wish you never came to the bar that day when we were kids, Med. Not for me, for you. It put you on his radar. He said he hadn't seen your Mom for years before that day. I remember him asking me about you that night. He said you were sin sent to punish him. I was so busy watching the game I didn't really pay attention to him but I should have known. Over the years he would say weird shit about you." He looks lost as he speaks. He gazes at Beats who is cradling herself on the floor.

I reach for her, lifting her into my arms. "When did you speak to Dad, I thought he was AWOL?"

"He was. He said he couldn't bear what she had done to me, making me give up football, so he left to make plans."

"I want to see him. None of this makes sense. I want to hear it from him."

Max is sitting at the table with his mouth open. "You can take her to my room," he says to me. "I have an en-suite. Go get her sorted. "He walks over to Justin. "I can't believe what I've just heard. I want you out. You've lost your fucking mind."

I take Beats to the bathroom, putting her down on the side of the bath. I turn on the tap and wet a cloth. She looks up at me with her tear-stained face.

"God, Rift. What did I turn him into?" Her voice is barely a whisper.

I swipe her face with the cloth. "Don't do that, Beats. Dad turned him into that. I should never have left Justin there with him. Fuck, this is crazy. I don't know what to do."

"I need to get home to my girls. I need to be near them."

"Our girls."

Her eyes shine with unshed tears. As they penetrate into mine a small smile tilts her lips. "Ours."

She reaches her arms around my neck to bring me to her. I wrap her in my arms and inhale her scent. "I love you, Beats, and I loved the girls even when we thought they weren't mine. To find out they are, God, I feel complete. We were always meant to be together. You were made for me. Marry me, baby?"

She pulls away to look me in the eyes, her mouth popping open.

"Are you serious?" she whispers.

I look around, realizing the time and place suck, but I can't help the need to put a ring on her finger and bind her to me forever.

"I know the time and place could have been better, but it's what I feel that matters. I want you now and forever. I want us to be husband and wife, I want to make more babies and finally be together properly as a family with our girls."

She throws herself into me, making me brace myself before relaxing into her body. "I want that too. Yes, I'll marry you."

My heart expands, tightening against my chest. I squeeze her tighter. Fuck, I love this woman. "Call Crystal. Tell her to keep the girls overnight. I want to take you somewhere. The girls are already asleep. We can be there for when they wake up."

"Okay," she agrees, pulling her phone from her jeans. I leave her to make the call and walk back into the living space to see Justin packing his bag.

"I could never truly hate you, Justin. You are my brother and I should have never left you, but I can't change the past. I know you think I don't deserve to have Beats, but I love her. She's going to be my wife like she was always meant to be. I'm grateful you picked up the pieces and took care of her when I left, but that didn't make her yours. She was always mine. We are soul mates and I know that's hard for you but you need to move on so one day maybe you can be a part of the girls' lives. We're family and I love you. I hate some of the things you have done. I hate that you got a piece of her heart but I hate myself for giving you the opportunity too. I'll never leave her again, not even in death."

A variety of emotions cross his face. "Take care of them," is all he says as he slings the bag over his shoulder and leaves the apartment.

Beats' footsteps pull me from my gaze.

"She said that's fine, so where are we going?" she asks.

MEADOW

I LOOSEN MY grip from around Rift's waist as the bike rolls to a stop. He hops off and helps me to slide off. My ass is a little numb from the vibrations of the engine and being on the bike for a few hours.

I stand and rub my hands over my backside, gaining a chuckle from Rift. "Your ass will get used to it eventually. Come here, let me rub that fine ass better for you."

I grin as his hands grope my ass. He groans as his lips fall on mine, nipping at my bottom lip.

My nipples stand to attention, rubbing on the lace of my bra. "Mmm, you taste good, but why am I standing in a field?" I mumble against his lips.

He pulls his lips from mine and grins, releasing my body from his tight grip. "The club owns a lot of land, and they've give us this to build your dream house."

I watch his lips move as he speaks but I'm not sure if I heard him right. "What?"

He smiles, bringing his arms back around me. "I've spoken to some of the boys I have in Edmond's construction and they say we could have it done within three months."

My mouth opens and closes a few times. "What about the cost? My house won't be worth very much, Rift," I tell him.

His brow furrows. "I don't want your money. It's already paid for."

I feel lightheaded and my stomach stirs. "What? How?"

He shakes his head at me. "I paid for it. I have savings. I earn good money and have never had reason to spend it until now, plus I get a discount on the work." He grins and drops kisses over my face.

"Rift, I need to know before we get married and I uproot mine and my girls' lives."

"Our girls," he corrects.

"Right. I need to know that you're not doing anything that will end with you locked up and me alone again."

His loud belly-clutching laugh resonates around me, and he tips his head back. He finally stops laughing when he notices my scowl. "Listen, I won't lie. Some of my work would be frowned upon but I'm really good at what I do. There's no chance I'd ever get locked up for any of the businesses I'm involved in. But I also should tell you that sometimes I have to do shit like protect my brothers or our club, and that could carry jail time, but I'll never be reckless and we have a lot of sway with the law here." He winks and although it terrifies me to think of what those things are that could carry jail time, I can't condemn him for protecting his family. This club is his family. "Beats, I can't tell what you're thinking but I see your lip being chewed by your teeth and I know that means you're thinking, but you will be my wife no matter what. There's no way in hell I'll ever let you go again."

I pull from his hold and cock an eyebrow. "Don't tell me, Rift. I won't be told what to do by any man. I might have to go find me a new man," I joke putting my hands on my hips for effect. The look in his eyes darkens, making me swallow. He clearly doesn't find me funny.

He comes so close to my face, his breath lifts the hair from my cheek. "I will kill any man that goes near you. Don't joke about shit like that. You and my girls belong to me and I belong to you. I waited long enough to claim you and now I have, I'll never let you go."

I feel butterflies take flight in my stomach. Even though what he said is possessive, I like that he is. "You make me sound like a prize you won."

"You are a prize, and I'm the luckiest son of a bitch in the world to win first place."

His lips crush down on mine and I willingly part my lips for him, taking his sweet tongue into my mouth and sucking him deeper.

He groans, eliciting a moan from me in return. His hands caress my back as he pulls me into him. I feel his erection against my stomach. His hands drop to my thighs, lifting me to wrap my legs around his waist.

My hard nipples brush against his chest, the fabric of my clothes becoming unbearable. "Fuck, Beats. I need to be inside you, baby," he groans against my lips, causing my panties to dampen. He walks us to his bike, straddling it with me still wrapped around him. His lips ascend to my neck, kissing and sucking at my soft skin. I continue to move my hips against him, causing friction that makes my core throb with anticipation.

He reaches for the hem of my shirt, lifting it from my body, the cool night air tantalizing my sensitive skin. His hands caress the prize he's exposed, grazing over my bare stomach. He pulls his lips from my neck to tell me I'm beautiful before he pulls the cups down of my bra, exposing my taut nipples. His hot mouth closes over one nipple while his hand cups the other, rolling his palm across the tightened bud. I feel my body ignite with need.

"I need inside you," he growls.

He leans me back against the handle bars and rips at the button on my jeans, popping it open and unzipping me, ripping them down my body, exposing my bare sex. "Shit, you're glistening for me, baby."

I tilt my pelvis up to him as he speaks his words, getting wetter with every breath I take. He pulls at the buttons on his jeans and springs free, his cock making me pant with appreciation. Pulling me up flush against his body he lowers me down onto his shaft, entering me slowly. His mouth hovers open over mine as I moan and pant; his teeth clamp down on my bottom lip as he fully enters me. His eyes gloss over with desire and it awakens the pure raw need for him in me.

I lift my body up feeling his hard cock leave my body and then I slam back down onto him hard, gyrating my hips in a powerful circle motion, grinding myself deep onto him before rising and dropping back down. His hands grip my hips as I continue my aggressive assault.

He tilts me back so his hot mouth can devour my breasts. I put both hands behind me holding myself up as I continue to lift my hips up and down his hard shaft. His hands and mouth touch every inch of bare skin.

He lifts my leg up in front of him and stands so he can push forward into me harder. He kisses my ankle as he thrusts deep powerful movements inside of me.

"Oh God, Rift!"

He whips me up and directs me to turn over so my ass is in the air and my bare breasts are pushed against the leather seat. "Grab the handle bars, baby, and don't let go."

I oblige, gripping my hands over the bars tightly and resting my feet on the floor to give me some balance. His hands splay across my bare ass as he leans forwards to kiss down my back. He drops his hand between my legs to find my throbbing clit: teasing with gentle circles, his finger sliding above and around my clit. He then brushes over the needy nub, tormenting me, bringing me to the brink of ecstasy as my chest heaves.

I feel my core boil and tighten. "I'm going to come," I moan, and he wastes no more time. He tilts my ass up and plunges deep inside, making me cry out as my body explodes around him. He thrusts into me hard a few more times before pulling free, spilling his seed all over my ass and lower back, coating me with his warmth before dipping back inside to empty the last drop.

My body feels weak. I loosen my hands from the handlebars and jump a little when Rift smacks my ass then bites my ass cheek. "I said not to let go," he growls, with a smile in his voice.

"I thought you had finished." I giggle. He wiggles his hips, causing me to shudder.

"I'm still inside you, aren't I?"

"Mmm, yes you are."

He chuckles and squeezes my hips. "You look fucking unreal naked across my bike, Beats. You're a wet dream come to life." He slips himself from me, leaving me feeling empty without him buried deep inside. He pulls my back against his chest, one arm holding me across my breasts the other around my waist, my back to his front. "I fucking love you, baby."

We stay like this for a few minutes before he squeezes me and shifts his body from the bike. "Get dressed, baby. This place is secluded but there is the occasional car that passes."

I gasp and grasp my clothes from the floor. "I thought it was private property," I tell him, angry that he just had me naked and splayed across his bike with the chance someone could have drove past. I know this isn't the first time we've been flippant about doing this outside, but I was drunk then, I don't have the shots making me brave this time.

"It is, but the road leads to other developments." He opens his saddle bag and pulls out a folder. "Here's the design for the house. If you don't like anything, we need to get it changed now so work can start."

I open the folder to see the plans for our house. "Four bedrooms?" I ask.

"Yeah, I want more babies to fill our house with." The glimmer in his eyes makes my heart swell.

"What's this?" I ask, pointing to a smaller structure near the main house.

"It's a guest house for Crystal." He cups my face in both his hands. "I know how close you are, and the girls adore her. I was hoping she would move with us."

A tear escapes from my eye. "She will love this. Thank you," I breathe. He pulls me into his embrace and I feel a vibration pulse up my leg. I arch an eyebrow and look up to him. "Is that a new super power your cock has?" I ask with a grin.

His face beams back at me and we both chuckle. He pulls his cell from his jeans and darkness crosses his features. He swipes his finger over the phone and growls into the receiver. "What? When?" I watch him pace and my inside begins to twist into an uncomfortable knot. He flips the phone shut and looks over to me. "Let's go, babe."

He gestures towards his bike. I stop him from getting closer to the bike by standing in his path. "Who was that?"

"No one. Come on, let's get home to our girls."

I hear my phone chirping and Rift becomes still like a statue. I reach into my jeans for my phone and see Justin's name. I swipe over the screen, bringing the phone to my ear. "Hey," I whisper hesitantly.

"I didn't know he was that unstable, Med. I had nothing to do with this."

My stomach drops. "What? What do you mean?"

His harsh breathing sounds like I'm on the freeway with the window open. "Justin!"

Rift snatches the phone from me. I look at him in shock. "He took your Mom, Beats."

I step back. "Who? What do you mean took her?"

"Our Dad, he's lost the plot. Drew's been trying to get in contact with us all. Yesterday he come home to a smashed up bar from signs of a struggle and your Mom is missing."

I shake my head. "That doesn't mean your Dad took her, that could mean anything," I mutter, still in shock.

"Justin had a message from him. He has her."

I don't know what I feel. I haven't spoken to my Mom in two years and the last time was when she chose to protect Jared's Dad.

A cold shiver slices through me. "What did the message say?"

His face looks haunted. I step closer, my fists clenched tight. "TELL ME!"

"That she deserves to be punished, and he can't risk her getting the girls."

My heart slows. I can hear every beat like a death march in my ears. "What does that mean, Rift?" He shakes his head and tries to pull me to him. I struggle against him. "We need to get home to the girls now," I say, pulling free and running to the bike, throwing my leg over.

We pull up at the curb next to my house; the sun is just creeping over the horizon. Rift's phone buzzes as I leap from his bike. He answers and I wait nervously to know who it is.

"Where the fuck are you?" His eyes shift to me as he speaks. "Fine, where?" He ends the call and looks to me. "I have to go somewhere, I won't be long. I love you."

Before I can argue, he revs his bike and takes off. I stand there watching his silhouette disappear from view.

I take a deep breath and run up the steps to my house, fishing my key from my pocket. I put it up to the door and noticed it's ajar. My heart plummets as I slowly pushed the door open. My mind screams at me to not panic but I'm a parent, and my babies are inside.

I run straight in, skidding to a halt when I see Crystal on the floor, her face bruised, and blood trickling from her mouth. I check her pulse and cry with relief when I find it.

Standing, my eyes go to the stairs where my babies should be sleeping. My whole body shakes as I ascend the stairs. Fear condenses, the air thickening it. It cloaks me in its cruel hold, staining my soul and consuming my heart.

I reach their door. Exhaling, I reach for the handle. Before I can open it I hear mine open behind me. I turn and tremble as Rift's Dad comes into view. He bolts forward, grabbing my hair and smacking my head into the door frame of the girls' room. I cry out as white specks play across my vision. A warm liquid seeps down my face as he tugs me backwards. I fall in a heap. His heavy body comes crashing down, covering mine and pinning me to the floor.

Memories from Justin's bathroom overflow my memory and I whimper. "Please don't."

His answering laugh is harsh and inhuman. "I want you to stand up and come with me, without a struggle, to my car." His breath burns my face as the smell of whiskey steams from his mouth.

"Why would I do that?"

"Because if you don't, I will kill you and take the girls instead."

My body shudders and tears form and spill over. I would never risk them. "Okay, okay. Just let me see them first. Please!"

He lifts from me, dragging me up with him, twisting his hand into my hair at the nape of my neck so he can guide me like a puppet. He turns the door knob of the girls' door and it swings open. Both girls are sleeping peacefully, their chests rising and falling evenly. Relief washes over me but it's fleeting. I need to keep them safe and get him away from them. He tugs my hair tighter, making me whimper.

"Down the stairs."

I obey, taking one step at a time, trying not to fall. I watch in horror as Crystal stirs, praying he didn't see her movement.

He rushes me from the house and down the path. I notice the black sedan and realization hits me. He was the stalker that was following me. He walks around to the trunk and pops it open. "Get in," he orders, pushing me forward. Dread grips me, infesting my body and I freeze. "GET IN!" he bellows, lifting me and forcing me inside. The darkness closes in around me, swallowing me. My whole body shakes as my mind runs through several outcomes but they all come back to my babies having to grow up without me.

The vibrations from the car's movements let me know how far

we travelled away from my babies. My heart cries out as I think about Rift getting back to find me gone. My body is weak when we finally come to a stop, the tremors have left me tired and dazed.

I hear footsteps approach and then light blinding me as the trunk opens. Hands reach in, gripping my arms and pulling me from the car. I land in a heap at his feet, the concrete bruising my knees with a thud. I notice we're in a garage. He grasps my hair roughly. I put my hands up as a reflex, grabbing his wrist to try and loosen his hold on me, but to no resolve.

I'm pulled up to my feet, whimpering at the pain in my head where he holds me. A fire roars in my nerves. His hand gropes my breast roughly. My hand immediately drops there, trying to push him away but he overpowers me, grabbing my hand, twisting at the wrist and causing a sharp pain to shoot up my arm. His face comes close to mine as he breathes heavy across my lips, and his tongue snakes out, wetting them. Vomit threatens as tears sting my eyes.

I push my lips together as tight as possible and he laughs. "You really are sin, you little dick-teasing whore." He yanks me forward towards a door, opening it, dragging me up a flight of stairs and through a dingy kitchen into a dark hallway.

He opens a door and forces my head through the opening. "Say hi to Mommy," he growls. My eyes flicker up to see my Mom naked, beaten and tied to a bed. My legs give out and I collapse to the floor as a sob wracks through my body. I knew he was a sick bastard but I never really allowed my mind to process just how bad he could have been if he had gotten away with what he wanted every time he cornered me. Yet, here I am, bleeding, in pain, and completely at his mercy.

I feel his breath against my ear. "Don't feel sorry for her, she likes it rough. She was the one who introduced me to the painful pleasure side of sex like the good whore she is."

Dragging me back to my feet and closing the door, he shoves me forward, guiding me to another door and pushing me inside.

There is a bed and nothing else. It's barren with bare white walls.

My mind explodes when I realize what he's going to do to me. More tears leak onto my cheeks as I cower away from him. He reaches for me, grasping me by my belt loop. "No, no, no, no, no, no," I chant. I feel like the little girl he trapped in the bathroom.

It's like I'm looking at the devil himself. "Don't worry, Justin wants dibs on you first then I get my turn, and you'll be saying yes, yes, yes."

My head feels fuzzy. "Justin?" I whisper, confused.

He pushes me backwards, the back of my knees colliding with the bed. I fall down onto the bare mattress. "You teased him for years. I had no idea you never gave it up to him. You fucking owe him and me, flaunting that body around and denying us. Your mother made you into the perfect whore just to punish me."

"I don't understand. Why would she want to punish you?" I whimper.

He grunts at me. "Because I knew the devil sent her, but I left her, stopped her from doing his work. She wanted me to raise you as mine." He laughs. "She came to town when she was sixteen, three months pregnant and still flaunting her ass around. She tried to trap me with her pussy but I wasn't stupid, I wasn't going to let some tramp hold me down. I knew I could live my life, marry a lady, but still get my thrills from your mother because she liked to offer it out freely. But then when you started growing up, she moulded you to be like her; to tease and lure my boys, seduce them as punishment for me not marrying her and not raising you as mine. She wanted me to have to look at you every day so you could tease me and not be allowed to touch you." He leans down to me, "And then as you got a little older she turned you onto me anyway, taunting me with your tight body."

I flinch and try to cover myself even though I'm fully clothed. "I took what I wanted from her but then she married my loser brother and tried to deny me, and you lied to my son to make him hate me. You ruined him just like I knew you would. He gave up everything

BECAUSE OF YOU!" he roars in my face, bringing his hand down hard across my cheek. The impact makes my vision blur, the mark turning to fire. I hear a ringing in my ear as unbearable heat burns the cheek he struck. I look at him with disgust and rage roaring through me. I kick out, hitting him in the stomach with my foot. He lets out an oof sound and doubles over.

I charge at him, knocking him to the ground, and attempt to run past him. Grabbing my ankle he tugs hard. I fall forward, my hands slapping the floor as I land, creating a sting in my palms and the earlier injury from him twisting my hand. He climbs me like a commando climbing a rope, grabbing at my clothes and flesh, pulling his full weight onto me. He grips my hair at the nape of my neck, lifting my head and slamming it down. The impact sends me into instant darkness.

I PULL MY bike up at the address he gave me, then pull out my phone and call Ice. He picks up after two rings. "What do you need?" he asks. I never ring Ice unless I have a job for him.

"I need you to make your way here. I might need you to clean for me."

"Personal or business," he asks, not that he will care. He only asks so he knows whether to involve any of the other brothers. "Just you, personal."

"Leave your phone on, I'll GPS it."

I end the call and slip my gun from the side satchel into the back of my jeans. The place looks abandoned. I'm cautious of my surroundings. The fact that no one's around and its deserted makes me edgy.

My heavy footsteps echo around the abandoned development as I slowly walk up the path to a beat down house. My phones vibrates with Justin's name flashing on the screen.

"What?"

"Tell me you're with Meadow." His voice is strained.

"No, Dad called me wanting to talk, I'm like an hour from hers at some run down street. I dropped her off first. Why?"

"He's fucking lost it. He's insane." His voice is weak, like he's struggling. "I had a message from him saying that he's going to give me what she flaunted for too long before he kills her."

The break in his voice makes me swallow.

"What the fuck does that mean? He has her Mom. Does he mean her Mom?" My voice is laced with anger.

I run up the pathway and kick the rotting wooden door open. It crumbles under my weight, dust and dirt lift from the floor as it disintegrates. The house is empty, undisturbed for what seems like years. My stomach drops. "Where is he? Why did he make me come here?" I whisper down the phone, but I already know the answer. "He led me away from her. Fuck!"

"I'm on my way to you, Jared. I'll be a few hours though. Shit, he's changed his phone. I can't get in touch with him!"

I end the call and bring Beats' name up in my phonebook. I hit the ring icon and bring it to my ear. The endless ringing brings dread creeping into my bones. I hear the connect and my heart jumps until I hear her answer machine. "Sorry I missed your call. Please leave your details and I'll get back to you." Her voice washes over me like warm caramel over ice cream, melting my heart. I can't lose her.

I rush back to my bike and take off in the direction of Beats' house. I try Crystal's phone and get no answer. I grip the handlebars and blast the engine, my mind playing havoc with me as the miles pass. I finally reach her street, the flashing lights from a police car and an ambulance sends ice shooting through my veins.

I jump from my bike, leaving it to crash to the floor. I rush past the crowd that has gathered and push my way through. "No sir, please stay back," an officer says. I ignore him, fear driving me forward. He grabs at me and I shrug him off easily. More officers rush at me.

"That's my family in there!" I roar as I barge them out of the way. I see Crystal standing in the passage, a paramedic trying to calm her down. Our eyes meet and she sprints towards me. "God

Rift, I'm sorry. Someone took her, he forced his way in and hit me with something and I was coming around when I saw her being forced out the door."

"Where are the girls?"

She gestures towards the house. "They're okay, the paramedics are checking them over but they're fine. My Mom's coming to get them. They want me to go hospital because of my head injury."

I pull her to me and squeeze her tight. "You should go then, but get back to my girls as soon as you can and look after them until I bring their Mom home." I kiss the side of her head and walk away. I can't see my girls right now, my body is running on adrenaline and I'm ready to put my Dad in the ground.

I hear the cops' voices calling to me but I don't stop for them. I take out my phone and call Digger.

"Yo, what's up brother? You coming home yet?"

"My Father has kidnapped Beats. I need you all."

I end the call, pick up my bike and take off. I drive for an hour before I reach my destination. The black iron gates open as I approach. The winding drive leads me to a huge white house. The door opens before I cut the engine and Kristy, Samuels little sister bursts through it, her pixie cut hair bouncing around her face. She's wearing only a satin wrap; her bare legs show as she jumps. She looks around me down the drive and pouts. "Didn't you bring me my toy to play with?" Samuel is a friend of the club, he knows computers, like code is written in his blood. He got me Beats address from just her phone number within an hour. He and his sister are both a little depraved, Ice usually comes with us to keep her occupied and sated when we have club business but this isn't a social call.

"This isn't business or fun, Kristy. I need your brother. Is he here?"

She turns and crooks her finger for me to follow. Our footsteps echo down the marble foyer. She opens a huge oak door to Samuel's office and she saunters over to him. He's sitting behind an oak desk, bashing away at a keyboard. He doesn't look up until Kristy drops into his lap and strokes his hair. Their relationship is not the usual brother/sister relationship but he is the best at what he does so most people overlook the fact he's banging her.

"Rift, I wasn't expecting you," He looks behind me. "Alone?" he asks and I nod.

"Hmm, is that why you're in my lap, Kristy?"

She pouts. "He didn't bring my toy."

"I need you. My Father finally cracked, he's taken my woman and her Mom."

Kristy stops her mauling and stands. Rushing over to me she throws herself into my arms and whispers against my cheek. "Oh no, poor baby."

Her Father is the reason she and her brother are so fucked up.

"Leave us, Kristy."

She saunters from the room and I move closer to the desk. "Why has he done this?" he asks.

"He blames her for Justin giving up football, and it came to light that he has tried to get physical with her before, with force." I bite out the last bit, my whole body screaming for me to find her. A dark shadow falls over Sam's face.

"What do you need?" he asks.

"I have no clue where he is or where he's been. I need you to hack everything that has his name on it." He nods and I collapse into the seat opposite his desk.

A couple of hours pass and I'm pacing, feeling completely useless, but I know Sam's my best chance. He can do things the police can't and he's a genius when it comes to computers, hence the mansion he lives in. His skill pays well.

"I'm into his computer," he says. I rush around the desk and lean over his shoulder.

"How the fuck do you do that?"

He grins. "He has a sharing program. People think they're harmless but it leaves your computer files open for others to see and use. I hacked in through that and can see everything he has."

He opens a file named Sin. My stomach twists as images of Beats flicker onto the screen; her from years ago, all through her teens, some with her sleeping next to me at his house, and then more recent ones.

Shit, he's been stalking her. A picture of me between her thighs on my bike at the bar lights up the screen next. Sam raises his eyebrows but he keeps clicking and then stops when he sees one of her beaten and bleeding on a bare mattress. He groans, and I realize I'm crushing his shoulder under my hand. "He just uploaded this one."

He opens more files, bank accounts and shit. I shake with anger and fear of what he's doing to her.

Another hour passes and I'm losing it. I can't bear not knowing where to find her. The door opens and my brothers pile into the room.

"What the fuck happened?" Digger asks.

I fill them in on everything and we wait. "I've activated the camera, his webcam is now on, on his laptop" Sam announces.

I waltz over to him and look into the screen. My Father is sitting at a table holding a gun, and he looks jumpy. I watch him stand and pace then walk down a hallway that leads from the kitchen, where his laptop appears to be on a table. He stops at a door, opens it and looks in, then shakes his head and hits himself a couple times like he's having an internal debate. My stomach twists into knots.

He walks into the room and I scrunch my hands into fists, struggling not to kill someone. He emerges minutes later holding a pair of jeans in his hand. Beats was wearing jeans. I bring my hands up to my face and scrub them down over my eyes. He sits back down and brings the jeans to his face, inhaling them.

"There's a phone there but he doesn't have one registered to him and it's not your girl's. I traced hers to her own address," Sam tells us.

"Maybe it's one of those ones you can't trace. You know, the fifteen dollar ones from gas stations?" Ice asks.

"It's too fancy to be one of those."

"What's her Mom's name? Maybe it's hers?"

We watch him pick the phone up and make a call. It lasts only a few minutes, then my phone rings.

"Justin."

"Where the fuck are you? I just pulled up at Meds' house and he called! He's five minutes from here. I'm going there now. I'll text you the address. Meet me there, Jared." He ends the call and my hands begin to shake. She was five minutes away and I drove away again. I'm an hour from her now.

My phone beeps and the text from Justin with the address lights up the screen. We all rush out, the roar of our bikes vibrate the ground as we ride away.

Justin

I'M SHAKING AS I drive to the address Dad gave me. I can't believe how far he's gone. I always believed Jared and Meds embellished where my Father was concerned, until he came to me with the plan to mess with the DNA results, and yet I let him convince me. I just wanted to cling to something. I've always been left and abandoned, and I just wanted to give back some of the hurt I've felt over the years. I'm fucked up too. I've fallen so far.

My stomach rolls as I come to a stop outside a small house. The shutters are closed on all the windows and it's secluded compared to the other houses in the block. I turn off the engine and step from the car then take a deep breath and walk up the steps to the front door.

It opens when I get to the top and my Father is standing there looking tired. He has black circles under his eyes and his hair is a mess, like he's been running his hands through it.

He waves me in, holding a gun in his hand. I enter and the door clicks shut behind me. He marches me up the hall and opens a door. There's a bed with no bedding on it, just Meadow laid across it in her panties and a top. Her face is bruised and there's dried blood in her hair and down her face. Scratches and bruises mark her thighs, and I fight the bile rising in my throat. She's shivering and my head buzzes with hurt and anger that he has done this to her.

I look at him and he shakes his head. "I haven't touched her like that yet. I was waiting for you. She's my gift to you," he tells me, pleased with himself.

I struggle to believe he is the same man who raised me. I see him twitch his finger over the trigger and I step forward. "Where's her Mom?"

"She owed me," he states, fully believing his statement. He gestures to another door.

"I want to be alone with Meadow," I tell him and he smiles.

"Okay, but I get her when you're done. She wants me, too. She's always wanted me, Justin. That's why she toyed with you and your brother for all these years, to make me jealous, to drive me crazy."

He has gone so far off the deep end I'm scared of him.

"We can take what she offers up then we'll kill them both so they can't turn your girls into whores." He smiles and walks up the hallway.

I close the door to the bedroom and rush over to Meadow. She pulls her knees up to her chest and scurries away from me. "It's me, Meds. Fuck, did he touch you?"

Little sobs shake her body and I grab her to me. "No, no, no," she whimpers and my heart breaks. How could I not see how twisted he was? She was always afraid of him and I ignored the signs.

"Med, look at me. Can you walk?" I move some hair from her face.

"Justin, why?" she murmurs.

I hold her for a while until her body calms a little. She needs a hospital and I need to get the gun from him and get her to one. I lay her back down and go to the door. I hear him pacing. I open the door and step into the hallway. "I need some water."

He nods and points to the fridge. I open the door and pull out a bottle of spring water. I look him over, stopping at the gun in his hand. "You can put that down Dad," I tell him.

He shakes his head. "I need it. She's sin, Justin. She will try to trick me if I don't have it. She pretends she doesn't want me."

My grip tightens on the bottle. I hear the low hum of bikes approach and I feel relief for a fleeting moment. My Dad's eyes flare wide with hatred.

I rush past him to go to Meadow. As I enter the room and go towards her, a loud popping from a gunshot rings through the apartment. I turn and hear his footsteps stomp in our direction. Meadow jumps up from the bed and clings to my back. "What was that?"

My Dad's frame fills the doorway. "We need to end it now," he growls.

Meadow backs away from me and curls into herself, sliding down the wall behind me. My Dad steps into the room and raises the gun towards her; my heart thuds against my chest. It feels like time slows as I watch his finger twitch. I jump in front of Meadow as a spark flashes and I feel a burning sensation ignite through my chest.

MEADOW

JUSTIN DROPS TO the floor in front of me and I scream. I rush to him. Shaking, I put my hand over his chest. The blood dampens his shirt, spreading like a broken ink pen bleeding onto a page. Tears blur my vision as I hear a loud thud and voices filter through the house.

"What the fuck?"

Rift has entered the room, and his Dad is still standing there with the gun pointed towards me. Rift takes a quick step, bringing a fist to the side of his Dad's face. He falters, dropping the gun, and falls to the floor.

Rift runs to me and cups my face as he slips his shirt off and puts it over my head. I take my hands from Justin's chest to quickly slip my arms in, then I put them back over his wound. "Did he touch you, baby?"

I hear the crack in his voice. I know what he's asking. I shake my head and relief washes over his features. He moves my hands from Justin and rips Justin's shirt, exposing the wound. There's a small hole in his chest; blood is pumping from it, making me heave.

He balls up the shirt and holds it tight to the wound. I hear movement and see their Dad get to his feet. I panic and reach for the gun, gripping it in my hand. I point it at him. "Don't move," I choke out.

Ice enters the room quietly behind Markus.

"Give me the gun, baby. We is going to take care of him. Give me the gun," Rift coaxes.

I shake my head and continue to hold up the gun in my shaky hand. Tears cascade down my cheeks.

"He won't ever leave me alone until he has me," I sob as my arms burn from holding them up. I feel so weak. Ice moves forward, his hands go to Jared's Dad's head. It's so quick. I flinch from the crack it makes as he twists, breaking his neck. His body falls to the floor like lead. Ice steps over him and walks towards me.

"Give me the gun, sweetheart. He's gone. He won't ever get you again."

I blink at the ice blue eyes staring into mine. I release the gun into his hand. He turns to Rift.

Sirens sound in the backround. "Turn your head sweetheart," Ice tells me and I do. I hear a shot ring out into the room and I shake with fear.

"He killed himself," I hear Rift tell me.

I open my eyes to see Ice putting the gun next to the lifeless body that now has a hole in the side of the head. I hear voices fade out as the sirens come closer. Minutes pass then the room fills with police officers and paramedics.

MEADOW

THEY SAY IF it rains when someone dies, its heaven opening the doors for their soul. There was no rain that day.

I feel the warm hand of Rift grip mine as I look down the six foot hole.

Drew told us that their mother was an extreme catholic who suffered with a mental break down when their Father left her for a younger woman. Drew went with his Father to live but Mr Jacobs, Rift's Dad, stayed with their mother who told him women are whores who would be sent from the devil to corrupt him, with sin, she told him one would be sent to test him, to taunt him.

He believed my Mom was the whore and I was the sin. He was crazy, and I have the scars in my memory and a couple on my body that will stay with me forever to prove it.

The police told me he was the one who friend requested me on Facebook, using a fake account in Justin's name. That was where he got my address and details from. Social media stalkers paradise.

*

"You ready, baby?"

I'm ready. I drop the rose I was holding down the hole onto my Mom's coffin and let Rift lead me away.

Justin suffered a collapsed lung and huge blood loss but he pulled through. He put himself through some intense counselling at a medical facility and is coming to terms with everything that happened.

The police didn't question the death of Mr Jacobs after I told them he killed himself. Although they did an investigation the results confirmed my side of the story, he wasn't around to dispute it. I follow Rift to his bike, his lips dropping to mine. He pulls away and whispers, "You ready to start our life, baby?"

I smile and throw my leg over his bike.

Epilogue

MEADOW

"HE'S HERE, THEY just arrived," Crystal informs me.

Justin had got delayed. He had to drive instead of fly because Ellie, the waitress from Drew's bar who gave him shit all those years ago, is now carrying his baby and didn't want to fly.

"You look amazing," Crystal says.

I look down at the red dress I picked out; it is Rift's favorite. I smile, looking down at his wedding ring on my finger. We waited four months before we got hitched. Our home had just been built and we wanted to move in as husband and wife; that was two years ago.

Jules and Jasmine come running into the room, "Uncle Justin's here, Mommy," Jasmine mumbles. She's been struggling with her speech since she lost a front tooth in play care when one of the other kids hit her in the face with a bottle because she wouldn't share her lunch. Needless to say, that boy's Father is also missing a tooth and has had it drilled into him to teach his boy never to hit girls.

I hurry the girls from the side room used to store crap in and enter the club. It's packed with all our family and they are all silent. Keeping a room full of hard ass bikers, their women and their kids quiet is not something to be taken lightly.

The door opens and my gorgeous man fills the space of the door frame. "Surprise!" We all scream and he jumps. He actually jumps.

I rush over to him. "Happy birthday, baby," I say.

"Holy shit, I nearly had a heart attack." He squeezes me against him.

"I signed the deed on the studio today." I beam up at him. He had bought me my own studio as a surprise for my birthday. It's small but perfect for starting out. He had my original red Fender restored and framed behind the desk, while my black one took pride of place in its stand in the recording room.

"Would you like to unwrap your gift now or later?" I ask seductively. He looks over at everyone smiling at him then back to me, pulling away, his eyes rake slowly over my body.

"Now." He grabs my hand and marches me up the stairs to everyone hollering and catcalling us, then the music plays and their voices filter out.

He rushes me into his old room. I bite my lip as he stalks towards me. "I love that fucking dress, baby."

I giggle. "I know."

"Lift it to your waist," he orders. I shake my head and he cocks an eyebrow. "No?"

"I need you to take it off. Unwrap me, your gift is underneath."

He grins and turns me around, gathering my hair and scooping it over my shoulder to kiss the bare skin exposed at the nape of my neck. "You smell fucking divine."

His fingers slide the zipper on my dress, slowly lowering it, tracing kisses down my spine as he uncovers bare skin. When he reaches the top of my ass the dress drops, pooling at my feet. "What's this?" he asks. His fingers stroke the ribbon tied around my waist.

Turning me around to face him, he sucks in a breath at the bow sitting over my belly button. "For real?" he asks.

I grin. "I found out last month but I didn't want to tell you straight away." His eyes narrow. We've been trying to get pregnant ever since we got married, and I was starting to worry until I felt sick and went to the doctor to be told I was three months pregnant. I didn't even have a bump, my stomach was flat. He told me that was perfectly normal and I could be carrying low in my back, and it was also normal to still have a light period in my first couple of months. Rift was away at the time, so I held out for the fourth month to find out what we're having to surprise him for his birthday.

He looked down at the ribbon. "How far along?"

"Four months," I murmur.

"Is there a reason this ribbon is blue?"

I bite my lip and nod. His face lights up, his eyes sparking.

"Holy shit, you got my boy in there?"

He picks me up, spinning me around, his head burrowing into my neck. "Happy birthday, Rift," I whisper.

Carrying me over to the bed he makes slow intense love to me.

We have everything. Each other, two beautiful girls, and now a boy on the way. Justin is happy and settled, and finally content with me being with Rift. He said he likes to see the light back in my eyes.

He's right; the light is back because Rift is my light, my soul mate, and I am The Beat in Rift.

The End

Keep reading for a sneak peek at upcoming works

Façade

A Dark NA Romance erotica

D.H SIDEBOTTOM & KER DUKEY

Coming soon

Synopsis for Façade

You meet someone. You date. You fall in love. You marry.

The four simple rules of love….
Wrong! I'm married but I'd never met him before now, never dated him, never fell in love. I have no access to the memories of the most magical time of anyone's life.

My mind won't allow me to evoke the past, I can't remember those four simple stages.

I can't comprehend why I would have ever married someone like Dante. I should never have passed the first stage, although, I may have seen him through the eyes of the woman I once was, this me that lives, breathes here now, can't understand how we made it to the next stage.

I'm not sure, without memories, how I know that this voice inside me, telling me I would never have chosen him, speaks some truth, I just know. He's controlling, arrogant, callous and violent, and utterly hell bent on humiliating and degrading me – Like watching me falter, watching me struggle to comply and be the woman he married, powers him- as though he wants to break me piece by piece. Fibre by fibre. Until all that's here is the shell he created from a soul that I once owned.

Now my memories are slowly returning. And they show me a completely different side to meeting him. Our dates, falling in love. The Dante haunting me in the shadows of my mind is loving, gentle and utterly enamoured with me, nothing like the man with me now.

And this is what taunts me. My tender lover turned into a debauched, cruel sadist who is determined to consume my life, destroy my mind and murder my spirit.

I am, Star, and just like with some stars in the sky, the light you see is an echo, a façade, I am already gone

I am a no one.

Especially to him. To him I am the dark in his desires, the corrupt in his depravity.

The sin in his immorality.

A snippet from upcoming novel

Empathy

by KER DUKEY

Blake

I've never hesitated before, I kill without remorse.

The girl who loves me, Abby, the one I fuck and leave because I don't have feelings for her, I just enjoy the pleasures of her body, the warmth she lets me into, she's a psych major and says I have psychopath tendencies. She says I have a deficiency in empathy. She cried at me one night, telling me I lack the emotions to care about anyone. But if that was true why do I care about my brother? And why when the single tear that dropped from the green eye and the *live* tattoo on the wrist of the little spitfire girl that nearly knocked herself out running into me earlier at Ryan's college, would make me hesitate in this moment? Why did seeing her in the mirror stun me when I recognised her, make me not want to squeeze my fist tight around her neck, ending the inconvenience of this cluster fuck of a job?

Of all the coincidences this one blew my mind. The aroma of her body flared the life of the man in me when it hit my nose. She was scared and shaking, the sweat carrying her scent to me, making me become human in a time I needed to be the Evil I was born to be, created to be what the fuck ever.

"You fucking coward, at least face me if you're going to kill me," She murmured.

Pride, hell I was proud of her in that moment and that was a new feeling for me, she wasn't as weak as I first thought.

My anger grew, I didn't want to feel anything, I needed to kill her.

This job had turned bad so fast it was a shit storm that might have me tracking the client who hired me and killing him for fun. No one was supposed to be here except the parents, and it was supposed to be a quick, clean kill while they were asleep. An alive girl and two dead people in a mass of blood and gore in the dining room was not how I wanted to leave this house.

I had no choice now, I spun her around and forced her head back into the mirror knocking her unconscious. It shattered and splintered around her like confetti.

She was beautiful, I was cold-hearted not blind. She lay there with her hair fanned out around her, her mind at peace. She would never feel it if I just ended her life right now, but I couldn't. I stalked back into the shadows and waited and watched as she arouse from her temporary slumber. Why I stayed I will question for my entire life.

When I broke I didn't see it, I felt it though.

When I kill I don't think about the person I kill, the family they might have or the person who has to find the bodies. So to watch first hand as a girl awakes from a dream to be forced into a nightmare and watch her break right in front of me is a surreal moment, it's an uncomfortable experience for me. I can't work out what this is I'm feeling.

It's visible, a person's soul fracturing. You see their world collapse, their beliefs leave them. You see the raw grief switch to anger, the why has this happened to me transform their features. Then the shutters closing over their eyes, their soul dimming their light. The darkness, the cold, evil taking them hostage, altering them forever, the slouch of the shoulders, and the drop of the mouth. The color of their skin turning pale. You see the anger, grief and disbelief rage in their eyes like a storm at sea before it calms to an empty ocean, just

For news, updates and teasers come join me on Facebook
https://www.facebook.com/KerDukeyauthor

Email here at
kerdukey@gmail.com

https://twitter.com/KerDukeyauthor

Add me on good reads
https://www.goodreads.com/book/show/18619029-the-bro-
ken?ac=1

Other works by Ker Dukey

THE BROKEN

THE BROKEN PARTS OF US

Made in the USA
Charleston, SC
02 October 2015